POUL ANDERSON

"The shock at the end, after the action, when you suddenly realize that you've been cheering the wrong side, or the weaklings aren't, or some basic law has been ignored ... the color, smell, taste of an alien world, a nonhuman society, a globular cluster or the universe seen from the very edge of lightspeed ... these things Poul shows better than anyone."

—Larry Niven

"Everybody 'knows' that Poul Anderson is one of the best: they're wrong—<u>he's better!</u>"

J.E. Pournelle

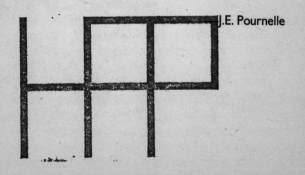

The Psychotechnic League...

Cold Victory

POUL ANDERSON

With a Foreward and
interstitial material by
Sandra Miesel

TOR

A TOM DOHERTY ASSOCIATES BOOK

COLD VICTORY

Copyright © 1982 by Poul Anderson

A TOR BOOK

First printing, March 1982

ISBN: 0-523-48527-1

Cover illustration by Vincent DiFate

Printed in the United States of America

PINNACLE BOOKS, INC.
1430 Broadway
New York, New York 10018

Acknowledgements:
The stories contained herein were first published and
are copyright as follows:

"Quixote of the Windmill", *Astounding*, ©1950 by
Street & Smith, Inc.;

"Brake", *Astounding*, ©1957 by Street & Smith, Inc.;

"Holmgang" (as "Out of the Iron Womb"), *Planet Stories*,
©1957 by Love Romances Publishing Company

"What Shall It Profit?", ©1955 by Galaxy Publishing
Corporation

"Cold Victory", Venture Science Fiction, ©1957, by
Mercury Press, Inc.

CONTENTS

FOREWORD

The critical decades following World War III were years of chaos and stubborn courage. Looking back across the millennia at the colossal challenge our twentieth century ancestors faced, we must salute the sacrifices they made to restore their shattered world. While mourning the follies of violent ages gone by, we humans can take pride in this: after each disaster, our species keeps on striving, like a trampled plant once more struggling towards the sun.

Of course in this case as in all cases timing as well as determination influenced the outcome of events. If World War III had erupted much later than 1958, perhaps no amount of heroism could have saved civilization from extinction. As it was, the East-West exchange of "nuclear Christmas presents" left key areas of both sides in radioactive ashes. Local wars followed global war; plagues succeeded famine. Civilization spun down toward darkness.

The first spark of hope kindled in Europe when Valti's theories of sociosymbolic logic proved themselves in practice. We who take psychodynamics as much for granted as hyperlight physics may find it difficult to appreciate what those first crude equations meant. No longer would we stumble through each day as it came; the future could be adjusted to fit the common good. To insure this happy outcome, the Psychotechnic Institute was founded. It became the self-appointed torchbearer for our race.

The United Nations, revived by the First Conference of Rio in 1965, was an effective instrument for putting the Institute's discoveries into action. This intimate and largely fruitful collaboration continued for more than a century. Together the Institute and the world organization presided over the rehabilitation of Earth.

Their first task was to preserve the hard-won peace. Our initial volume, *The Psychotechnic League*, recounts four significant episodes in the process. Guided by the new social science, men with "dirty hands and clean weapons" destroyed potential dictators before irreparable harm was done. Sacrificing the few today on behalf of the many tomorrow was the ethic that shaped an era.

With the return of peace came plenty. Once people could safely grow food and produce goods again, output surpassed all expectation. Automated equipment compensated for population loss. Pent up demand following decades of want sent the postwar economy soaring. The need for alternative energy sources to replace those ruined by the war was met by solar power and synthetic fuels with superdielectrics for storage. Once power-beaming satellites went into orbit, Earth's energy worries seemed over.

Earth grew green again. There was a keen, well-nigh universal desire to preserve whatever beauty the war had spared and restore what it had ravished. Acute ecological awareness would soon inspire foundation of the Pancosmic religion, a faith that continues to attract many adherents, human and nonhuman alike.

Zeal for reclamation plus the practical experience gained from building undersea settlements prepared Earthlings to colonize the Solar System. Soon domed cities rose on Luna, the asteroids, and even distant Ganymede. Bold terraforming schemes made Venus and Mars habitable after nearly a century of heartbreaking toil. The independent Order of Planetary Engineers (originally the UN's Planetary Engineering Corps) distinguished itself in all these projects but the ''enterprise beyond the sky'' was truly a species-wide concern. Mere survival did not suffice: Mankind was out to leave its mark on the universe.

But the Psychotechnic Institute foresaw that this burst of energy would fade. Remolding worlds was simpler than remodeling humanity. While continuing to chart and influence the behavior of whole societies, the Institute also experimented with individuals. For a time, an elaborate holistic conditioning system known as Tighe Synthesis seemed an excellent way to maximize human potential. Although a few receptive subjects benefitted from the training, this promising discovery was never widely applied. Not only was it impractical to condition the entire population adequately, the process put too much power in the hands of the conditioners.

Yet despite its shortcomings, the science of psychodynamics was our margin of survival. Institute-trained personnel were indispensible in that first critical century following World War II. Foremost among these heroes were the UN-Men cloned from a *maquis* named Stefan Rostomily. (Humble, gifted, and steadfast, the Rostomily Brotherhood was destined to outlast the Institute that had created it.) United Nations agents were everywhere in those days but perhaps their most admirable feat—one which redounded to the Institute's credit—was the liberation of Venus from a bleak Stalinist tyranny in 2065. With the collective state gone, the colonists speedily developed a fiercely parochial clan-based society whose romantic folkways were celebrated in popular entertainment for generations afterwards. Political historians still analyze Venus as an experiment in local autonomy.

By the opening of the twenty-second century, the Psychotechnic Institute's power and prestige reached their zenith. The bright future it had planned for humanity seemed inevitable. High technology was triumphant. The blessings of the Second Industrial Revolution were available to all. No one went hungry or homeless any more. Work had become a privilege instead of an obligation. From sophisticated Earthlings to roughneck colonial, mankind shared a common, semantically rigorous language called Basic. The space navy of the newly-formed Solar Union stood guard from Venus to the Belt. The New Enlightenment bathed Sol's children in the cool radiance of reason.

But there were shadows. . . .

QUIXOTE AND THE WINDMILL

The first robot in the world came walking over green hills with sunlight aflash off his polished metal hide. He walked with a rippling grace that was almost feline, and his tread fell noiselessly—but you could feel the ground vibrate ever so faintly under the impact of that terrific mass, and the air held a subliminal quiver from the great engine that pulsed within him.

Him. You could not think of the robot as neuter. He had the brutal maleness of a naval rifle or a blast furnace. All the smooth silent elegance of perfect design and construction did not hide the weight and strength of a two and a half-meter height. His eyes glowed, as if with inner fires of smoldering atoms; they could see in any frequency range he selected, he could turn an X-ray beam on you and look you through and through with those terrible eyes. They had built him humanoid, but had had the good taste not to give him a face; there were the eyes, with their sockets for extra lenses when he needed microsopic or tele-scopic vision, and there were a few other small sensory and vocal orifices, but other-wise his head was a mask of shining metal. Humanoid, but not human—man's creation, but more than man—the first independent, volitional, nonspecialized machine—but they had dreamed of him, long ago, he had once been the jinni in the bottle or the Golem, Bacon's brazen head of Frankenstein's monster, the man-transcending creature who could serve or destroy with equal contempt-uous ease.

He walked under a bright summer sky, over sunlit fields and through little groves that danced and whispered in the wind. The houses of men were scattered here and there, the houses which practically took care of themselves; over beyond the horizon was one of the giant, almost automatic food factories; a few self-piloting carplanes went quietly overhead. Humans were in sight, sun-browned men and their women and children going about their various errands with loose bright garments floating in the breeze. A few seemed to be at work, there was a colorist experimenting with a new chromatic har-mony, a composer sitting on his verandah striking notes out of an omniplayer, a group

of engineers in a transparent-walled lab-
oratory testing some mechanisms. But with
the standard work period what it was these
days, most were engaged in recreation. A
picnic, a dance under trees, a concert, a pair
of lovers, a group of children in one of the
immemorially ancient games of their age-
group, an old man happily enhammocked
with a book and a bottle of beer—the human
race was taking it easy.

They saw the robot go by, and often a
silence fell as his tremendous shadow slipped
past. His electronic detectors sensed the eddy-
ing pulses that meant nervousness, a faint unease—oh, they trusted the cybernetics men,
they didn't look for a devouring monster, but
they wondered. They felt man's old unsure-
ness of the alien and unknown, deep in their
minds they wondered what the robot was
about and what his new and invincible race
might mean to Earth's dwellers—then,
perhaps, as his gleaming height receded over
the hills, they laughed and forgot him.

The robot went on.

There were not many customers in the Casanova at this hour. After sunset the tavern
would fill up and the autodispensers would be
kept busy, for it had a good live-talent show
and television was becoming unfashionable.
But at the moment only those who enjoyed a
mid-afternoon glass, together with some
serious drinkers' were present.

The building stood alone on a high wooded

ridge, surrounded by its gardens and a good-sized parking lot. Its colonnaded exterior was long and low and gracious; inside it was cool and dim and fairly quiet; and the general air of decorum, due entirely to lack of patronage, would probably last till evening. The manager had gone off on his own business and the girls didn't find it worthwhile to be around till later, so the Casanova was wholly in the charge of its machines.

Two men were giving their autodispenser a good workout. It could hardly deliver one drink before a coin was given it for another. The smaller man was drinking whiskey and soda, the larger one stuck to the most potent available ale, and both were already thoroughly soused.

They sat in a corner booth from which they could look out the open door, but their attention was directed to the drinks. It was one of those curious barroom acquaintances which spring up between utterly diverse types. They would hardly remember each other the next day. But currently they were exchanging their troubles.

The little dark-haired fellow, Roger Brady, finished his drink and dialed for another. "Beatcha!" he said triumphantly.

"Gimme time," said the big red-head, Pete Borklin. "This stuff goes down slower."

Brady got out a cigarette. His fingers shook as he brought it to his mouth and puffed it into lighting. "Why can't that drink come right away?" he mumbled. "I resent a ten-second delay. Ten dry eternities! I demand instantaneously mixed drinks, delivered faster than light."

The glass arrived, and he raised it to his lips. "I am afraid," he said, with the careful precision of a very drunk man, "that I am going on a weeping jag. I would much prefer a fighting jag. But unfortunately there is nobody to fight."

"I'll fight you," offered Borklin. His huge fists closed.

"Nah—why? Wouldn't be a fight, anyway. You'd just mop me up. And why should we fight? We're both in the same boat."

"Yeah," Borklin looked at his fists. "Not much use, anyway," he said. "Somebody'd do a lot better job o' killing with an autogun than I could with—these." He unclenched them, slowly, as if with an effort, and took another drag at his glass.

"What we want to do," said Brady, "is to fight a world. We want to blow up all Earth and scatter the pieces from here to Pluto. Only it wouldn't do any good, Pete. Some machine'd come along and put it back together again."

"I just wanna get drunk," said Borklin. "My wife left me. D'I tell you that? My wife left me."

"Yeah, you told me."

Borklin shook his heavy head, puzzled. "She said I was a drunk. I went to a doctor like she said, but it didn't help none. He said . . . I forget what he said. But I had to keep on drinking anyway. Wasn't anything else to do."

"I know. Psychiatry helps people solve problems. It's not being able to solve a problem that drives a man insane. But when the problem is inherently insoluble—what then? One can only drink, and try to forget."

"My wife wanted me to amount to something," said Borklin. "She wanted me to get a job. But what could I do? I tried. Honest, I tried. I tried for . . . well, I've been trying all my life, really. There just wasn't any work around. Not any I could do."

"Fortunately, the basic citizen's allowance is enough to get drunk on," said Brady. "Only the drinks don't arrive fast enough. I demand an instantaneous autodispenser."

Borklin dialed for another ale. He looked at his hands in a bewildered way. "I've always been strong," he said. "I know I'm not bright, but I'm strong, and I'm good at working with machines and all. But nobody would hire me." He spread his thick workman's fingers. "I was handy at home. We had a little place in Alaska, my dad didn't hold with too many gadgets, so I was handy around there. But he's dead now, the place is sold, what good are my hands?"

"The worker's paradise." Brady's thin lips twisted. "Since the end of the Transition, Earth has been Utopia. Machines do all the routine work, *all* of it, they produce so much that the basic necessities of life are free."

"The hell. They want money for everything."

"Not much. And you get your citizen's allowance, which is just a convenient way of making your needs free. When you want more money, for the luxuries, you work, as an engineer or scientist or musician or painter or tavern keeper or spaceman or . . . anything there's a demand for. You don't work too hard. Paradise!" Brady's shaking fingers spilled cigarette ash on the table. A little tube dipped down from the wall and sucked it up.

"I can't find work. They don't want me. Nowhere."

"Of course not. What earthly good is manual labor these days? Machines do it all. Oh, there are technicians to be sure, quite a lot of them—but they're all highly skilled men, years of training. The man who has nothing to offer but his strength and a little rule-of-thumb ingenuity doesn't get work. There *is* no place for him!" Brady took another swallow from his glass. "Human genius has eliminated the need for the workman. Now it only remains to eliminate the workman himself."

Borklin's fists closed again, dangerously. "Whattayuh mean?" he asked harshly. "Whattayuh mean, anyway?"

"Nothing personal. But you know it yourself. Your type no longer fits into human society. So the geneticists are gradually working it out of the race. The population is kept static, relatively small, and is slowly evolving toward a type which can adapt to the present en . . . environment. And that's not your type, Pete."

The big man's anger collapsed into futility. He stared emptily at his glass. "What to do?" he whispered. "What can I do?"

"Not a thing, Pete. Just drink, and try to forget your wife. Just drink."

"Mebbe they'll get out to the stars."

"Not in our lifetimes. And even then, they'll want to take their machines along. We still won't be any more useful. Drink up, old fellow. Be glad! You're living in Utopia!"

There was silence then, for a while. The day was bright outside. Brady was grateful for the obscurity of the tavern.

Borklin said at last: "What I can't figure is you. You look smart. You can fit in . . . can't you?"

Brady grinned humorlessly. "No, Pete. I had a job, yes. I was a mediocre servo-technician. The other day I couldn't take any more. I told the boss what to do with his servos, and I've been drinking ever since. I don't think I ever want to stop."

"But how come?"

"Dreary, routine—I hated it. I'd rather stay tight. I had psychiatric help too, of course, and it didn't do me any good. The same insoluble problem as yours, really."

"I don't get it."

"I'm a bright boy, Pete. Why hide it? My I.Q. puts me in the genius class. But—not quite bright enough." Brady fumbled for another coin. He could only find a bill, but the machine gave him change. "I want inshantaneous auto . . . or did I say that before?

Never mind. It doesn't matter." He buried his face in his hands.

"How do you mean, not quite bright enough?" Borklin was insistent. He had a vague notion that a new slant on his own problem might conceivably help him see a solution. "That's what they told me, only politer. But you—"

"I'm too bright to be an ordinary technician. Not for long. And I have none of the artistic or literary talent which counts so highly nowadays. What I wanted was to be a mathematician. All my life I wanted to be a mathematician. And I worked at it. I studied. I learned all any human head could hold, and I know where to look up the rest." Brady grinned wearily. "So what's the upshot? The mathematical machines have taken over. Not only all routine computation—that's old—but even independent research. At a higher level than the human brain can operate.

"They still have humans working at it. Sure. They have men who outline the problems, control and check the machines, follow through all the steps—men who are the . . . the soul of the science, even today.

"*But*—only the top-flight geniuses. The really brilliant original minds, with flashes of sheer inspiration. *They* are still needed. But the machines do all the rest."

Brady shrugged. "I'm not a first-rank genius, Pete. I can't do anything that an electronic brain can't do quicker and better. So I didn't get my job, either."

They sat quiet again. Then Borklin said, slowly: "At least you can get some fun. I don't like all these concerts and pictures and all that fancy stuff. I don't have more than drinking and women and maybe some stereo-film."

"I suppose you're right," said Brady indifferently. "But I'm not cut out to be a hedonist. Neither are you. We both *want* to work. We want to feel we have some importance and value—we want to amount to something. Our friends . . . your wife . . . I had a girl once, Pete . . . we're expected to amount to something."

"Only there's nothing for us to do—"

A hard and dazzling sun-flash caught his eye. He looked out through the door, and jerked with a violence that upset his drink.

"Great universe!" he breathed. "Pete . . . Pete . . . look, it's the robot! *It's the robot!*"

"Huh?" Borklin twisted around, trying to focus his eyes out the door. "Whazzat?"

"The robot—you've heard of it, man." Brady's soddenness was gone in a sudden shivering intensity. His voice was like metal. "They built him three years ago at Cybernetics Lab. Manlike, with a volitional, non-specialized brain—manlike, but more than man!"

"Yeah . . . yeah, I heard." Borklin looked out and saw the great shining form striding across the gardens, bound on some unknown journey that took him past the tavern. "They were testing him. But he's been running around loose for a year or so now— Wonder where he's going?"

"I don't know." As if hypnotized, Brady looked after the mighty thing. "I don't know—" His voice trailed off, then suddenly he stood up and then lashed out: "But we'll find out! Come on, Pete!"

"Where . . . huh . . . why—" Borklin rose slowly, fumbling through his own bewilderment. "What do you mean?"

"Don't you see, don't you see? It's *the robot*—the man after man—all that man is, and how much more we don't even imagine. Pete, the machines have been replacing men, here, there, everywhere. This is the machine that will replace *man!*"

Borklin said nothing, but trailed out after Brady. The smaller man kept on talking, rapidly, bitterly: "Sure—why not? Man is simply flesh and blood. Humans are only human. They're not efficient enough for our shiny new world. Why not scrap the whole human race? How long till we have nothing but men of metal in a meaningless metal ant-heap?

"Come on, Pete. Man is going down into darkness. But we can go down fighting!"

Something of it penetrated Borklin's mind. He saw the towering machine ahead of him, and suddenly it was as if it embodied all which had broken him. The ultimate machine, the final arrogance of efficiency, remote and godlike and indifferent as it smashed him—suddenly he hated it with a violence that seemed to split his skull apart. He lumbered clumsily beside Brady and they caught up with the robot together.

"Turn around!" called Brady. "Turn around and fight!"

The robot paused. Brady picked up a stone and threw it. The rock bounced off the armor with a dull clang.

The robot faced about. Borklin ran at him, cursing. His heavy shoes kicked at the robot's ankle joints, his fists battered at the front. They left no trace.

"Stop that,' said the robot. His voice had little tonal variation, but there was the resonance of a great bell in it. "Stop that. You will injure yourself."

Borklin retreated, gasping with the pain of bruised flesh and smothering impotence. Brady reeled about to stand before the robot. The alcohol was singing and buzzing in his head, but his voice came oddly clear.

"We can't hurt you," he said. "We're Don Quixote, tilting at windmills. But you wouldn't know about that. You wouldn't know about any of man's old dreams."

"I am unable to account for your present actions," said the robot. His eyes blazed with their deep fires, searching the men. Unconsciously, they shrank away a little.

"You are unhappy," decided the robot. "You have been drinking to escape your own unhappiness, and in your present intoxication you identify me with the causes of your misery."

"Why not?" flared Brady. "Aren't you? The machines are taking over all Earth with their smug efficiency, making man a parasite—and now you come, the ultimate machine, you're the one who's going to replace man himself."

"I have no belligerent intentions," said the robot. "You should know I was conditioned against any such tendencies, even while my brain was in process of construction." Something like a chuckle vibrated in the deep metal voice. "What reason do I have to fight anyone?"

"None," said Brady thinly. "None at all. You'll just take over, as more and more of you are made, as your emotionless power begins to—"

"Begins to what?" asked the robot. "And how do you know I am emotionless? Any psychologist will tell you that emotion, though not necessarily of the human type, is a basic of thought. What logical reason does a being have to think, to work, even to exist? It cannot rationalize its so doing, it simply does, because of its endocrine system, its power plant, whatever runs it . . . its emotions! And any mentality capable of self-consciousness will feel as wide a range of emotion as you—it will be as happy or as interested—or as miserable —as you!"

It was weird, even in a world used to machines that were all but alive, thus to stand and argue with a living mass of metal and plastic, vacuum and energy. The strangeness of it struck Brady, he realized just how drunk he was. But still he had to snarl his hatred and despair out, mouth any phrases at all just so they relieved some of the bursting tension within him.

"I don't care how you feel or don't feel," he said, stuttering a little now. "It's that you're the future, the meaningless future when all men are as useless as I am now, and I hate you for it and the worst of it is I can't kill you."

The robot stood like a burnished statue of some old and non-anthropomorphic god, motionless, but his voice shivered the quiet air: "Your case is fairly common. You have been relegated to obscurity by advanced technology. But do not identify yourself with all mankind. There will always be men who think and dream and sing and carry on all the race has ever loved. The future belongs to them, not to you—or to me.

"I am surprised that a man of your apparent intelligence does not realize my position. But—what earthly good is a robot? By the time science had advanced to the point where I could be built, there was no longer any reason for it. Think—you have a specialized machine to perform or help man perform every conceivable task. What possible use is there for a nonspecialized machine to do them all? Man himself fulfills that function, and the machines are no more than his tools. Does a housewife want a robot servant when she need only control the dozen machines which already do all the work? Why should a scientist want a robot that could, say, go into dangerous radioactive rooms when he has already installed automatic and remote-controlled apparatus which does everything there? And surely the artists and thinkers and policy-makers don't need robots, they are performing specifically human tasks, it will always be *man* who sets man's goals and dreams his dreams. The all-purpose machine is and forever will be—man himself.

"Man, I was made for purely scientific study. After a couple of years they had learned all there was to learn about me—and I had no other purpose! They let me become a harmless, aimless, meaningless wanderer, just so I could be doing something—and my life is estimated at five hundred years!

"I have no purpose. I have no real reason for existence. I have no companion, no place in human society, no use for my strength and my brain. Man, man, do you think *I* am happy?"

The robot turned to go. Brady was sitting on the grass, holding his head to keep it from whirling off into space, so he didn't see the giant metal god depart. But he caught the last words flung back, and somehow there was such a choking bitterness in the toneless brazen voice that he could never afterward forget them.

"Man, you are the lucky one. *You* can get drunk!"

   *Perhaps the self-aware robot really was as
much a victim as the displaced workers, but
few humans cared to waste pity on its kind.
Outbreaks of anti-robot rioting signalled
growing public disenchantment with their
automated Eden. Mankind does not live by
bread—or citizen's credit—alone; abundance
may be harder to endure than scarcity.*
   *A few malcontents booked passage on the
first starship, the famous "slowboat to
Centauri." But whatever hopes they may have
cherished of escaping social turmoil faded en
route. Being human, they carried the trait for
conflict within them like an uncorrectable
genetic flaw.*

THE TROUBLEMAKERS

A bright dream, and an old one—the same dream which had lived in Pythias, Columbus, Ley, in hundreds and thousands of men and in man himself, and which now looked up to the stars.

Earth was subdued; the planets had been reached and found wanting; if the dream were not to die, the stars must come next. It was known that most of them must have planets, that the worlds which could hold man were numbered in the millions—but the nearest of them was more than a lifetime away. Man could not wait for the hypothetical faster-than-light drive, which might never be found—nothing in physics indicated such a possibility, and if the vision of the frontier, which had become a cultural basic transcending ques-

tions of merely material usefulness, were not to wither and die, a start of some kind must be made.

The Pioneer, *first of her class, was launched in 2126. A hundred and twenty-three years to Alpha Centauri—five or six generations, more than a long lifetime—but the dream would not be denied . . .*

—Enrico Yamatsu, *Starward!*

"Have you anything to say before your sentence is passed?"

Evan Friday looked around him, slowly, focusing on all the details which he might never see again. Guilty! After all his hopes, after the wrangling and the waiting and the throttled futile anger, guilty. It hadn't even taken them long to decide; they'd debated perhaps half an hour before coming out with the verdict.

Guilty.

Behind him, the spectators had grown silent. There weren't many of them here in person, though he knew that half the ship must be watching him through the telescreens. Mostly they were officer class, sitting stiff and uniformed in their chairs, regarding him out of carefully blanked faces. The benches reserved for crewfolk were almost empty—less color in the garments, more life in the expression, but a life that despised him and seemed to feel only a suppressed glee that one more officer had gotten what was coming to him.

There were five sitting before him, judge and jury in full uniform. Above them, the arching wall displayed a mural, a symbolic figure of Justice crowned with a wreath of stars. The woman-image was stately, but he thought with bitterness that the artist had gotten in a hint of sluttishness. Appropriate.

His eyes went back to the five who were the Captain's Court. They were the rulers of the ship as well, the leaders and representatives of the major factions aboard. Three were officers pure and simple, with the bone-bred hauteur of their class— Astrogation, Administration, and Engineering. The fourth was Wilson, speaking for the crew, a big coarse man with the beefy hands of a laborer. He was getting fat, after five years of politics.

Captain Gomez was in the center. He was tall and lean, with a fine halo of white hair fringing his gaunt unmoving face. You couldn't know what he was thinking; the loneliness of his post had reached into him during his forty-three years as master. A figurehead now, but impressive, and—

Friday licked his lips and drew himself up straighter. He was twenty-four years old, and had been schooled in the rigid manners of the Astro officer's caste throughout all that time. Those habits held him up now. He was surprised at the steadiness of his tones:

"Yes, sir, I would like to say a few words.

"In the first place, I am not guilty. I have never so much as thought of bribery, sedition, or mutiny. There is nothing in my past record which would indicate anything of the sort. The evidence on which I have been convicted is the flimsiest tissue of fabrications, and several witnesses have committed perjury. I am surprised that this court even bothered of finding me guilty, and can only suppose that it is a frameup to cover someone else. However, there is little I can do about that now. My friends will continue to work for a reversal of this decision, and meanwhile I must accept it.

"Secondly, I would like to say that the fact of my being falsely accused is not strange. It is a part of the whole incredible pattern of mismanagement, selfishness, treachery, and venality which has perverted the great idea of this voyage. The *Pioneer* was to reach the stars. She carried all the hopes of Earth, ten years of labor and planning, an incredible money investment, and a mission of supreme importance. Eighty years later, what do we have? An unending succession of tyrannies, revolutions, tensions, hatreds, corruptions— all the social evils which Earth so painfully overcame, reborn between the stars. The goal has been forgotten in a ceaseless struggle for power which is used only to oppress. I have said this much before, in private. Presumably some right of free speech still exists, for I was not arrested on such charges. Therefore, I repeat it in public. Gentlemen and crew, I ask you to think what this will lead to. I ask you in what condition we will reach Centauri, if we do so at all. I ask you to consider who is responsible. I know it will prejudice my personal cause, but I make a solemn charge of my own: that two successive Captains have failed to exercise due authority, that the Captaincy has become a farce and a figurehead, that the officers have become a tyrant caste and the crew an ignorant mob. I tell the whole ship that something will have to be done, and soon, if the expedition is not to be a failure and a death trap.

"If this is sedition and mutiny, so be it."

He finished formally: "Thank you, gentlemen." The blood was hot in his face, he knew he was flushing and was angry with himself for it, he knew that he was shivering a little, and he knew that his words had been meaningless gibberish to the five men.

But the crew, and the better officers—?

Gomez cleared his throat, and spoke dryly: "I am sure idealism is creditable, especially in so young a man—provided that it is not a cover for something else, and that it is properly expressed. But there is also a tradition that junior officers should be seen and not heard, and that they are hardly prepared to govern a ship and seven thousand human beings. The court will remember your breach of discipline, Mr. Friday, in reviewing your case."

He leaned forward. "You have been found guilty of crimes which are punishable by death or imprisonment. However, in view of the defendant's youth and his previous good record, the court is disposed to leniency. Sentence is therefore passed that you shall be stripped of all title, honor, and privilege due to your rank, that your personal property shall be sequestered, and that you shall be reduced to a common crewman with assignment to the Engineering Section.

"Court dismissed."

The judges rose and filed out. Friday shook his head, trying to clear it of a buzzing faintness, trying to ignore the eyes and the voices at his back. A police sergeant fell in on either side of him. He thrust away the arm which one extended, and walked out between them.

The gray coverall felt stiff and scratchy against his skin. They had given him two changes of clothing and a couple of dollars to last till payday, and that was all which remained to him now. He went centerward between the policemen, hardly noticing the walls and doors, shafts and faces.

The cops weren't bad fellows. They had looked the other way while he said good-bye to his parents. His mother had cried but his father, drilled into the reserve expected of an officer, had only been able to wring his hand and mutter awkwardly: "You shouldn't have spoken that way, Evan. It didn't help matters. But we'll keep working for you, and—and— good luck, my son." With a sudden flaring of the old iron pride: "Whatever happens, and whatever they say, remember you are still an officer of Astrogation!"

That had hurt perhaps most of all, and at the same time it had held more comfort than anything else. An officer, an officer, an officer—before God, still an officer of Astro!

It embarrassed the policemen. He was their inferior now, a plain crewman to be kicked around and kept in order, but he was of the Friday blood and he kept the manners they were trained to salute. They didn't know how to act.

One of them finally said, slowly and clumsily: "Look, you're in for some trouble, I'm afraid. Can you fight?"

"I was taught self-defense, yes," said Friday. Fitness was part of the code in all of Astro—which, after all, was composed exclusively of officers—as it was of only the upper ranks in Engineering and hardly at all in Administration. It belonged to the pattern; Astro was the smallest faction aboard, but it was the aristocracy of the aristocracy and at present it held the balance of power. "Why do you ask?"

"You'll have quite a few slugfests. Crewmen don't like officers, and when one gets kicked downstairs to them they take it out on him."

"But—I never hurt anybody. Damn it, I've been their friend!"

"Can't expect 'em all to see it that way. But stand up to 'em, be free and friendly—forget that manner of yours, remember you're one of them now—and it'll come out all right."

"You mean you police permit brawling?"

"Not too much we can do about it, as long as riots don't start. You can file a complaint with us if somebody beats you up, but I wouldn't advise it. They'd never take you in then. Somebody might murder you."

"I won't come crawling to anybody," said Friday with the stiffness of outrage. Underneath it was a horrible tightening in his throat.

"That's what I said: you've got to quit talking that way. Crewmen aren't a bad sort, but you can't live with 'em if you keep putting on airs. Just keep your mouth shut for awhile, till they get used to you."

The three men went down unending corridors, shafts, and companionways. Gravity lightened as they approached the axis of the ship. From the numbers on doors, Friday judged that they were bound for Engineering Barracks Three, which lay aft of the main gyros and about halfway between axis and top deck, but pride wouldn't allow him to ask if he was right.

They were well out of officer territory now. The halls were still clean, but somehow drabber and dingier; residential apartments were smaller and poorly furnished; shops, taverns, theaters and other public accommodations blinked neon signs at the opposite wall, fifteen feet away; the clangor of metalworking dinned faintly in the background. Crewfolk swarmed here and there, drab-clad for work or gaudy for pleasure, men and women and a horde of children. Most of the men wore close haircuts and short beards, in contrast to the clean-shaven officers, and they were noisy and pushing and not too clean.

Many of them looked after the policemen and
cursed or spat. Friday felt unease crawling
along his spine.

"Here we are."

He stopped, and looked ahead of him with a
certain panicky blurring in his eyes. The doorway, entrance to one of the barracks for un-
married workers, was like a cave. The other
doors on that side of the corridor, as far as he
could see, opened into the same racketing
darkness; the opposite wall was mostly blank,
with side halls and companionways widely
spaced. Two or three men, shooting dice some
way down the corridor, were looking up and
he saw their faces harden.

"We could go in with you," said one of the
police apologetically, "but it'll be better for
you if we don't. Good luck—Mr. Friday."

"Thank you," he said. His voice was husky.

He stood for a moment looking at the door.
The crapshooters got up and started slowly
toward him. He wondered if he should bolt in,
decided against it, and managed a stiff nod as
the strangers came up.

"How do you do?"

"What's the trouble, jo?" The speaker was
big and blocky and red-haired. "Been
boozin?"

"Nah." Another man narrowed his eyes.
"This's that guy Friday. The one they broke
today. They sent 'em down here."

"Here? Friday? Well, I'll be scuttered!" The
first crewman bowed elaborately. "Howdedo,
Mister Ensign Friday, howdedo an' welcome

to our humble *ay*-bode."

"Mebbe we sh'd roll out a rug, huh?"

"How'd y' like y'r eggs done, sir, sunny side up 'r turned?"

"Please," said Friday, "I would like to find my bunk." He recognized the condescending coldness in his voice too late.

"He'd like to find his bunk!" Someone grinned nastily. "Shall we show 'im, boys?"

Friday pushed himself free and went into the barracks.

It was gloomy inside, for a moment he was almost blind. Ventilators could not remove the haze of smoke and human sweat. Bunks lined the walls in two tiers, stretching enormously into a farther twilight. Pictures, mostly of nude women, were pasted on the walls, and the walls, and the floor, while not especially dirty or littered, was a mess of shoes, clothes, tables, and chairs. Most of the light came from a giant-size telescreen, filling one wall with its images—the mindless, tasteless sort of program intended for this class—and the air with its noise. Perhaps a hundred men off duty were in the room, sleeping, lounging, gambling, watching the show, most of them wearing little but shorts.

Friday had been "crewquartering" before with companions of his age and class, but he'd stuck to the bars and similar places; his knowledge of this aspect had been purely nominal. It was a sudden feeling of being caged, a retching claustrophobia, which brought him around to face the others. They had followed him in, and stood blocking the doorway.

"Hey, boys!" The shout rang and boomed through the hollow immensity of the room, skittered past the raucousness of the tele-screen and shivered faintly in the metal walls. "Hey, look who we got! Come over here and meet Mister Friday!"

Eyes, two hundred eyes glittering out of smoke and dark, and nowhere to go, nowhere to go. *They're going to beat me up. They're going to slug me, and I can't get away from it, I'll have to take it.*

He raised his voice above the savage jeering as they pressed in: "Why do you think I was sent down here? Why did they want to get rid of me, up above? Because I wanted you people to have some rights. I never hurt a crewman yet. Damn it, I couldn't have, I was always working with other officers."

"Here's your chance," grunted somebody. "I'll take him."

They squabbled for awhile over the privilege, while two men held Friday's arms. The big redhead who had first accosted him won.

"Let him go, boys," he said. "Give him a chance to in-tro-juice himself proper like. I'm Sam Carter, Mr. Friday." His teeth flashed white in the smoky dusk. "And I'm very pleased to meet you."

"Chawmed, I am shu-ah," cried a voice, anonymous in the roiling twilight.

Friday had learned the techniques of

boxing, wrestling, and infighting in all gravities from zero to Earth. He had enjoyed it, and been considered better than average. But Carter outmassed him thirty pounds, and officers didn't fight to hurt.

After awhile Friday lost fear, forgot pain, and wanted nothing in all the world but to smash that red grinning face into ruin. Up and down, in and out, around and around, slug, duck, guard, slug, jar, and the mob hooting and howling out of the shadows. Hit him, right cross to the jaw, left to the belly, *oof!*

It took Sam Carter a long time to knock him down for good, and the crewman was hardly able to stand, himself, when it was done. There wasn't much cheering. A couple of men hauled Friday to a vacant bunk, and went back to whatever they had been doing before he came.

Slowly, Friday adjusted.

At first it was not quite real, it was a horror which could not have happened to him. He, Ensign Evan Friday, rising in Astro, minor social lion, all the ship before him—he, who meant to do something about correcting injustice when he had the power, but who knew he could wait and savor his own life, he just wasn't the sort of person who was accused and condemned and degraded. Those things happened to others, actually guilty in the struggle for control, or to the heroes of books from the Earth he had never seen—they didn't happen to *him!*

He came out of that daze into grinding nightmare. It took him days to recover from the beating he had had, and before he was quite well somebody else took him on, somebody whom he managed to defeat this time but who left him aching and hurt. Nevertheless, he was sent to work two watches after his arrival, and to the clumsiness of the recruit and the screaming of unaccustomed muscles his injuries were added.

Being ignorant of all shopwork, he was set to unskilled, heavy labor, jumping at everyone's shout with boxes, machine parts, tools, metal beams. Low gravity helped somewhat, but not enough—they simply assumed he could lift that much more mass, without regard to its inertia. His bewildered awkwardness drew curses and pay dockings. The racket of the shops seemed to din in his head every time he tried to sleep, and he could never get all the grime out of his skin and clothes.

Without friends, money, or a decent suit, he stayed in the barracks when the others went out to drink, wench, or see a show. But somebody was always around with him, and the telescreen was never turned off. He thought he would go crazy before he learned how to ignore it, but he knew better than to protest.

The men stopped bullying him after awhile, since he was disconcertingly handy with his fists, but it took weeks before the practical jokes ended. Shortsheeting and tying watersoaked knots in clothing were all right; he'd done that to others when he was younger; but hiding his shoes, pouring water in his bed and paint in his hair, slipping physics into his food—childish, but a vicious sort of childishness that made him wonder why he had ever felt sorry for this class.

He used the public facilities, bed and board and bath, since he could not afford the private home which theoretically was his to rent. He joined the union, since no one ever failed to, though it galled him to pay money into Wilson's war chest—Wilson, the parvenu, who wanted to run the officers that ran the ship! But otherwise he refused to conform, though it would have made things easier. He shaved, and kept his hair long, and fought to retain precision and restraint in his speech. He talked as little as possible to anyone, and spent most of his free time lying on his bunk thinking.

The loneliness was great. Sometimes, when he thought of his friends, when he remembered his quiet book-lined room, he wanted to cry. It was a closed world now. Crewmen simply didn't go into officer territory except on business.

Well, they might get him cleared. Meanwhile, the best thing he could do was to improve his position.

He worked with machines now and then, and was a little surprised to discover he had a fair amount of innate ability. Books from the crew branch of the ship's library taught him more, and presently he applied for promotion to machinist's assistant. By now he was tolerated, though still disliked, and made a good enough showing on test to get the job. It meant a raise, better working conditions, and one step further. The next was to be a machinist himself, one of the all-around men who were troubleshooters and extempore inventors—that was one grade higher than foreman, a job he could bypass.

Before God, he thought, *I'll get back to officer if I have to work my way!*

Theoretically, it was possible. But in practice there were only so many commissions to go around, and if you didn't belong to the right families you didn't get them.

He grew friendly with his immediate boss, a pleasant, older man who was not at all averse to letting him do most of the work and learn thereby. Gradually, he got onto drinking terms with a few others. They weren't bad fellows, not entirely the sadistic savages he had imagined. They laughed more than the upper classes, and they often went to school in their spare time, or saved money to start a small business, in spite of the disadvantages under which tradesmen labored.

For that matter, crew conditions weren't the slummish horror which sentimentalists had pictured. Folk were poor, but they had the basic necessities and a few of the comforts. Violence was not uncommon, but it was simply one facet of a life which, on the whole, was fairly secure. Indeed, perhaps its worst feature was dullness.

Still, if another of the minor wars which had torn the ship before broke out—Something was wrong. This wasn't the way man should go out to the stars, high of heart and glad of soul. Somehow, the great dream had gone awry.

It was a major triumph when Friday met Sam Carter in a beer hall and they went on a small bat together. He found himself liking the big red-headed man. And Carter got into the habit of asking him endless questions—science, history, politics; an officer was supposed to know everything. Friday began to discover how deficient his own education was. He knew physics and mathematics well, had a fair grounding in some other sciences, and had been exposed all his life to the best of Earth's art, literature, and music. But—what was this psychology, anyway? It was a scientific study of human behavior, yes, and it had advanced quite far on Earth by the time the ship left—but why had he never been taught anything but the barest smattering? For that matter, did anybody in the upper ranks ever speak of it?

That might be the reason why the ship's great dream had snarled into a crazy welter of murderous petty politics. Sheer ignorant fumbling on the part of the leaders, even with the best intentions—and he knew many intentions were and had been bad—could have let matters degenerate. Only—why? It would have been so easy to include a few psychologists.

Unless—unless those psychologists had been eliminated early in the game, say at the end of that serene first decade of travel, by the power-hungry and the greedy. But then the whole foundation of his society was rottener than he had imagined. Then even his own class was founded on betrayal.

None of which, he reflected grimly, was going to be any help at all when the ship got to Centauri.

If it ever did!

Perhaps still another revolution was needed, a revolt of the dreamers to whom the voyage meant something. Only—only there'd been too many mutinies and gang wars already, and more were brewing with every passing watch. The officers were split along departmental lines—Astros, Engys, and Admys—and on questions of personal power and general policy. The common crewfolk were nominally represented by Wilson, but some demon seemed to stir them up against each other, workers with machines and on farms, plain deckhands, technicians of all kinds of grades, hating each other and rioting in the corridors. Then there were the chants and small manufacturers, fighting for a return to the old free enterprise system or, at least, a separate voice on the Council. There were the goons maintained by each faction, as well as by powerful individuals, bully gangs outnumbering the better-armed police, who were directly under the Captain. But the Captain was a puppet, giving the orders of whatever momentary group or men held the reins of effective power.

*This ship isn't going to Centauri, thought
Friday. It's going to Hell!*

Time aboard the *Pioneer* was divided into the
days of twenty-four hours, the weeks of seven
and the years of three hundred sixty-five and
a quarter days, which had prevailed on Earth.
But except for a few annual festivals, there
were no special holidays. Working shifts were
staggered around the clock, and there was
always a certain percentage of the shops and
other public places open. For what meaning
did time have? It was the movement of clock
hands, the succession of meals and tasks and
sleeps, the arbitrary marks on a calendar. In a
skyless, weatherless, seasonless world, a
world whose only dark came with the flicking
of a light switch in a room, one hour was as
good as another for anything. The economic
setup was such that the standard thirty-hour
work week provided the common crewman a
living wage, and there was not enough work
to do for overtime hours to be usual. Most
people kept to such a schedule, and passed
their leisure with whatever recreation was
available and to their tastes. Some preferred
to work only part time and to do something
else for the rest of their money—one thought
especially of the *filles de joie* who, though
frowned on by the officer caste, were an
accepted part of the crew world; and the
arrogant goons were another instance. The
tradesmen, independent artisans, artists,

writers, and others who worked for themselves made their own hours. Some of these
lived in officer territory, the pet of a patron or
caterers to the entire area; most were in and
of the commons.

Evan Friday wandered with a couple of
friends—Sam Carter and a dark, slim, intense
nineteen-year-old named John Lefebre—into
Park Seven, not far aft of the main gyros. The
workers were idle, a little bored, and Friday
had wearied of spending too much time in the
library. He had been reading a good deal, con-
centrating on the history of the ship and
groping for the cause of its social breakdown,
but it baffled him and he was still young.

He had realized with a little shock that he
had been a crewman for almost six months.
So long? Gods, but time went, day after day of
sameness, days and weeks and months and
years till the end of life and flaming oblivion
in the energy converters. Time went, and he
was caught in its stream and carried without
will or strength. Sometimes he wondered if he
would ever get back to the topdeck world.
Increasingly it became dim, a dream
flickering on the edge of reality, and only once
in a while would its sharp remembrance bring
him awake with a gasp of pain.

He had shaken down pretty well, he
thought. He was accepted in the barracks,
though his reserve still kept most of the men
at a distance. But they called him "Doc" and
referred arguments to his superior education.
He was used to shop routine, learning fast

and getting close to the promotion he wanted. Next step—superintendent—maybe! He had been invited to the apartments of crew families, and went out drinking or gambling or ballplaying with the others. It wasn't too bad a life, really, and that was in a way the most horrible part of his situation.

They went down a long series of halls until finally one opened on the park. This was one of several such areas scattered through the ship, a great vaulted space half a mile on a side, floored with dirt and turf, covered with hedges and trees and fountains—a glimpse of old Earth, here in the steel immensity of the ship. There were ball courts and a swimming pool and hidden private places under fantastically huge low-gravity flowers. Not far from the boundary of grass were a couple of beer parlors—fun for all the family.

"Get up some volley ball?" asked Lefebre.

"Not yet," yawned Friday. "Let's sit for a while." He went his words one better, by flopping full length on the grass. It was cool and moist and firm against his bare skin, with a faint pungency of mould which stirred vague wistful instincts in him. His eyes squinted up to the ceiling, where the illusion of blue sky and wandering clouds and a fiery globe of sun had been created.

Was Earth like this? he wondered. Had his grandparents spurned this for a prison of steel and energy, walled horizons and narrow rooms and an unknowable destiny which they would never see?

He closed his eyes and tried, as often before, to imagine Earth. He had been in the parks, he had seen all the films and read all the books and learned all the words, but still it wouldn't come real. In spite of having ventured outside the ship a few times, he couldn't quite imagine being under a sky which was not a roof, looking out to a horizon that hazed into blue distance, seeing a mountain or a sea. Words, pictures, images—a fantasy without meaning.

Rain, what was rain? Water spilling from the sky, sweet and cold and wet on his body, damp smell of earth and a misty wind blowing into his eyes—whenever he tried to imagine himself out in the rain, it was merely grotesque, not the thing of which the books wrote with such tenderness. Someday, when he was old, the ship would reach far Centauri and he might stand under a streaming heaven and see lightning, but he couldn't think it now and he wondered if his old body would even like it.

It would take all the courage and purpose in the ship for men to adapt back to planetary life, the more so if the planet turned out to be very different than Earth.

What chance would a divided, tyrannized, corrupted mob have? What fantastic blindness had made Captain Petrie unable to see the spreading cancer and excise it? Or had he, like his successor Gomez, been merely the pawn and abettor of the greedy and the brutal? What had happened, back in the early days of the voyage? What had gone wrong?"

"What'cha thinking about now, Doc?" asked Carter.

"Hm? Oh—oh, the usual." Friday blinked himself back to full consciousness. "Remembering how things were when this trip began, and trying to find who or what's to blame for their changing ever since."

"Was—were things really so fine then?" asked Lefebre. "Aren't you, uh, romanticizing it?"

"No, no. I've read the official log, remember, as well as other writings. And it was only eighty years ago, not time for many legends to form."

"Well—what was so good then, anyway?" asked Carter.

"The ship was all one unit. Everybody had one great purpose, to get to Centauri, and everybody worked for it. There weren't these social divisions that have grown up since, officers and men were almost like friends, anybody could reach the top on sheer merit, nobody was after himself or his little group above the ship. There wasn't bribery, or fighting, or—oh, all the things which have happened ever since.

"Of course," went on Friday thoughtfully, "there were a lot fewer people then, and they had more to do. Only about two hundred in all, men and women. You know the population's supposed to build up and be at our maximum of ten thousand or so by the end of the trip. But we're only around seven thousand now, that'd be a small town on Earth—damn it, there's no reason for our splitting into castes and factions this way, it's ridiculous . . . Anyway, the ship was more or less of a skeleton inside, the idea was for the crew to complete work on it en route. That was so they could get started sooner, and have more to do. Good idea, and it took ten or twenty years at their easy pace."

"We still have to make things," said Carter. "What d'you think we're doing in the shops, anyway?"

"Sure, sure. Machines wear out and have to be replaced, repairs are needed here and there, new machines and facilities are built, oh, we have a whole little industry that keeps the factory division of the Engy department busy. Then there are the men in the black gang, different deck hands and technicians—we don't have the robot stuff we could make, there's no need for it with plenty of human labor available. My point is, things have stabilized. There's only so much work to be done these days, nearly all of it pure routine, so maybe people get bored. Maybe that's one reason we fight each other."

"The trouble started with capitalism," said Lefebre. He had all the dogmatic conviction of his years. "I've been reading books too, Doc, and heard speeches, and been thinking for myself. Any ship is a natural communist state. There was no reason to let private people have the farms and the factories and the rec places. What happened? Companies got started, fought each other, op—oppressed the workers, who had to form unions in self-defense; the food processors won out over the producers and formed their own trust; while Engy slowly took over the industries. Then food and factories started fighting, trying to run the ship, trying to stir up each other's workers—"

"So eventually the farms were collectivized, turned into one big food factory," said Friday. "Isn't that what you wanted? It hasn't helped much."

"The damage had already been done," said Lefebre. "The idea of fighting over power had been planted. Only thing to do now is to socialize everything, put it under the Captain's Council, and give the workers the main voice."

Friday had argued with the boy before. There was a strong communist movement aboard, chiefly under Wilson's leadership. *That fat demagogue! A lot of say his precious workers would have if he got what he wants!* Then there were the Guilds and their agitation for a return to the original petite-bourgeois system, their claim that the initial evil had been the formation of monopolies. And there were the officers, most of them obsessed by the artistocratic ideal, though to them it meant no more than the increase of personal authority and wealth.

Friday's upbringing prejudiced him in that direction. Damn it, a ship was not a politick-ing communism, neither was it a realm of

little, short-sighted tradesmen. It was the rule
of the best, the *aristos*, a hierarchy restrained
by law and tradition and open on a competitive basis to anyone with ability. But it had to
be an unquestioned rule, or you got the sort of
anarchy which had prevailed aboard the
Pioneer.

"To hell with it," said Carter. "Let's play
some ball."

They got up and strolled over to the courts.
The park was, as usual, pretty well filled with
crewfolk of all ages, sexes, and classes, gen-
erally dressed in the shorts which were the
garb of ordinary lounging. Except for the con-
venience of pockets, clothes were a super-
fluity when you weren't on the job. Friday
wondered how the arrivals at Centauri would
stand a winter—another half mythical con-
cept. Ship "weather" was a variation of
temperature and ozone balance in the cycle
long known to be most beneficial, but the
change was so slow and between such narrow
limits that it was unnoticeable. Winter—what
was winter?

There were several other Engys sitting on
the edge of the volley ball court, watching the
game in progress with sour faces. "What's the
matter, jo?" asked Carter of one.

"Goddam farmers been there for two hours
now."

With an uneasy tingle along his spine,
Friday noticed the characteristic green worn
by workers in the food areas—hyproponic
gardens, animal pens, and packing plants.

There were a lot of them, sitting some ways off and watching a game whose slowness made it clear that its purpose was to taunt the Engys by keeping the court occupied. Theoretically, the food and factory unions were subdivisions of Wilson's crew-embracing Brotherhood of Workers. In practice, a feud had been going on for—how long, now? Ever since the early violence in the days of the monopolies. It was aggravated by differences in wages, working conditions, the thousand petty irritations of shipboard life. They hated each other's guts.

"Something," said Carter after a while, "oughta be done about this."

He started forward with an unholy gleam in his eyes. Friday caught his arm. "For God's sake, Sam, you aren't going to fight like a bunch of children over the use of a ball park, are you?"

"Ain't busted in a farmer's teeth for him in a long time now," muttered someone behind him.

Friday saw the men gathering into a loose knot. Blackjacks and knuckledusters were coming out of pockets, heavy-buckled belts were being slipped off. The greens, seeing trouble afoot, vented the mob-growl which is the signal for all wise men to start running, and drew themselves together.

Unthinking habit took over, officer's training. Friday was dimly surprised to find himself sprinting out onto the court.

"Stop that!" he yelled. "Break it up!"

The players halted, one by one, and he met sullen eyes. "What'sa matter?"

"You've had your turn playing. Can't you see a riot will start if you don't come back now?"

Faces turned to faces, mouths split into the grin he remembered from his first hour as a crewman. "Well!" said somebody elaborately. "Well, well, well! Now isn't that just a dirty crying shame?"

He saw the fist coming and rolled, taking it on his shoulder. His own flicked out, caught the green in the jaw; stepping in close, he let the other hand smack its way into the muscled stomach.

The rest closed in on him, and he saw the gray ranks pouring onto the court to his rescue, and the greens after them. With a stabbing sickness, he realized that his own attempt had fired off the riot.

There was a swirl of bodies around him, impact and noise, metal flashing under the artificial sun. He slugged at short range, drowned in the shouting, frantic to get away. Taller than average he could look over the surging close-cropped heads and see more men on their way. The thing was growing.

Someone slapped at him with a blackjack. He caught the blow on an uplifted arm, numbing it in a crash of pain. Viciously, he kneed the man, yanked the weapon loose, and flailed the screaming face. A fist hit him in the side, he went down and the feet trampled over him. Gasping, he struggled erect, slugged out half blindly. The howling current bore him off without strength to fight it. Through a haze of sweat and panic, he saw knives gleaming.

"Back! Get out!"

The metal rod whistled around his head. He snarled incoherently and yanked it away. "I'm staying here," he mumbled.

"Get out, get out!" The man was screaming, a small frail gray-haired man with two women behind him. "Get out, we don't want you, you, you—rioter—"

Friday leaned against a counter, sobbing air into the harsh dryness of throat and lungs. A wave of dizziness passed through him, dark before his eyes and a distant roaring in his ears. No, no, that was the mob, screaming and thundering in the corridor outside.

A measure of strength returned. "I—not rioting—" he forced through his teeth. "Wait here—only wait here—"

"Why—father, he's no crewman. He's an *officer*—"

Friday let it pass. He found a chair and slumped into it, letting nerves and muscles recover. He noticed dimly that he had been slashed here and there, blood was pooling onto the floor, but it hadn't started hurting much yet.

"Here, take this."

The girl had brought him a glass of whiskey. He downed it in a grateful gulp, letting its vividness scorch down his gullet and run warmly along his veins. Awareness began to come back.

He had stumbled into a small shop, a poor
and dingy place cluttered with tools and
handicrafts. Plastics mostly, he noticed, with
some woodwork and metal, the small orna-
ments and household objects still produced
by private parties. Besides himself, there
were the man and his wife, and the girl who
must be their daughter. She was about nineteen or twenty, he thought in the back of his
mind, a slim blonde without extraordinary
looks but with a degree of aliveness in her
which was unusual.

The shopkeeper had locked the door by
now. Apparently the riot—and Friday—had
swept this way with a speed that took him by
surprise. He was close to tears. "They'll start
looting now," he said. "They always do. And it
isn't a strong lock."

"The police should be here soon," said
Friday.

"Not soon enough. I was looted once before.
If it happens again, I'm ruined, I'll have to
take a crew job—"

"You're hurt," said the girl. "Here, wait a
minute, I'll get the kit." Friday could barely
hear her voice above the echoing din of the
riot, but he watched her with pleasure.

Bodies surged against the plate window
until its plastic shivered. A man was backed
against it and another one swung a knife and
opened his throat. Blood blurred the view,
and the girl screamed and hid her face against
Friday's breast.

"I—I'm all right now," she whispered

presently. "Here, the bandages—"

He had to admire her. *He* still wanted to vomit.

The door shook. "They're trying to batter it down! They want to get in before the police arrive! Oh, God—"

Friday took the metal bar and went over to the door. He felt a vicious glee which was not at all proper to an officer and a gentleman. "You should keep a gas gun handy," he remarked.

"You know only officers are allowed weapons—but the bullies make their own—Oh, oh, help—"

The door broke under three brawny shoulders. Friday swung the improvised club with a whistle and a crack. The first man went down on that blow and did not move. The second, carrying a shaft of his own, raised it in guard. Friday, remembering his fencing, jabbed him in the belly and he screamed and stumbled back with his hands to the wound. The third one fled.

They had been greens, which was something of a relief. Friday would have fought grays as willingly, but that could have been awkard for him later, if he were recognized.

He felt a return of the sick revulsion. God, God, God, what had become of the ship? Why did anyone ever feel sorry for these witless, lawless animals? What they needed was an officer caste, and—

He heard whistles blowing and the heart-stirring cadence of marching feet. The police had arrived. He shoved his green victim—unconscious or dead, he didn't much care which—outside and closed the door. "Turn your fans on full," he said. "They'll be using gas."

"Oh, you—" The older woman sought for words. "You were wonderful, sir."

Friday preened himself, smiling at the girl, whose answering expression was quite dazzling. "Don't 'sir' me, please," he said, trying to find words which wouldn't sound too story-book silly in retrospect. "I'm only an Engy at present, though I've no use for rioters of any class." He bowed, falling back on the formal manners of topdeck. "Evan Friday, your servant, sir and ladies."

They didn't recognize the name, which disappointed him more than he thought it should. But he got their own names—William Johnson, wife Ingrid, daughter Elena—and an invitation to dinner next "day." He left feeling quite smug about the whole affair.

Paradoxically, the exhibition which had soured Friday on all crewmen led to his forming more friendships among them than ever before. Word spread that Doc had been in on the very start of the fight, been wounded, laid some undetermined but respectable number of greens low, and in general acquitted himself like a good Engy. Men struck up talk with him, bought him drinks, listened to his remarks—strange how warming a plain "hello" could be when he

came to work. He was more than merely
accepted, and in his solitude could not
prevent himself from responding emotionally.

Training told him that an officer and a
gentleman had no business associating with
any of these—these mutineers. Prudence, a
need of friends, and a growing shrewd
realization that if he hoped to accomplish
anything he would have to fit into the lower-
deck milieu, made him reply in kind. He
retained his eccentricities, haircut and shave
and faint stiffness of manner, noticing that
once his associates were used to these they
marked him out, made him something of a
leader.

His plans were vague. There had been no
word from topside, no word at all, though he
supposed his family was keeping track of him.
Once, in a tavern, he had encountered a group
of crewquartering young aristocrats, friends
of his, and his sister among them; there had
been an embarrassed exchange of greetings
and he had left as soon as possible. The upper
world was shut off. But if he could attain
some prominence down here, get influential
friends, money—Surely he couldn't remain a
crewman all his life! Such anticlimaxes just
didn't happen to Evan Friday.

He was doing a good deal of work in close
collaboration with the superintendent of his
shop. The intricacies of the job were resolving
themselves; he could handle it. He began to
speculate on ways of displacing his superior.

It did not occur to him that he might be pulling a dirty trick on another human being.

But something else was going on that distracted his attention. Strangers were dropping into the barracks, husky young men who, it became clear, were full-time attendants of Wilson—in less euphemistic language, his goons. They talked to various workers, bought drinks—recruited! Rumors buzzed around: there was a cache of weapons somewhere, there was this or that dastardly plot afoot which must be forestalled, there was to be a general strike for higher pay and better conditions of work and living. Certainly a young man could make extra money and have some fun by signing on as a part-time goon. You learned techniques of fighting, you drilled a little bit, you played athletic games and had occasional beer parties with old Tom Wilson footing the bill. It had been some time since the last pitched battle between goon squads, but by God, jo, those officers' men were getting too big in the head, strutting around like they owned the ship, it might be time to scutter them a bit.

"They wanted me to join," said Carter. "I told 'em no."

"Good man!" said Friday.

Carter ran a big work-roughened hand through his red stubble. "I ain't looking for trouble, Doc," he said. "I'm saving to get married." He scowled. "Only, well, maybe we will have to fight. Maybe we won't get our rights no other way. And if they did fight, and win, and I wasn't in on it, it'd look bad later on."

"That's the sort of gruff they've been feeding you, huh?"

"Well, Doc, you got a head on your shoulders. But—I dunno. I'll have to think it over."

Friday lay awake during many hours, wondering what was on the way. Certainly the other factions aboard knew what was going on—why did they allow it, then? Were they afraid to precipitate a general conflict? Or did they have plans of their own? Or did they think Wilson was merely bluffing?

What did the man want, anyway? He was on the Council already, wasn't he?

Couldn't they see—damn them, couldn't they see that the ship was bigger than all their stupid ambitions, couldn't they see that space was the great Enemy against which all souls aboard, all mankind had to unite?

A special meeting of the Brotherhood of Workers was called. Friday had only been to one union assembly before, out of a curiosity which was soon quenched by the incredible dullness of the proceedings. Men stood and haggled, hour after hour, over some infinitesimal point, they dozed through interminable speeches and reports, they took a whole watch to decide something that the Captain should have settled in one minute. He realized wryly that a major qualification of leadership was an infinite patience. And skill in maneuvering men, swapping favors, playing opponents off against each other, covering the operations that mattered with a blanket of parliamentary procedure and meaningless verbiage. But he had a notion that this meeting was one he should attend in person, not simply over a telescreen.

The hall was jammed, and the ventilators could not quite overcome the stink of sweating humanity. Friday wrinkled his aristocratic nose and pushed through to the section reserved for his grade, near the stage. He found a seat beside a friend with a similar job, and looked around the buzzing cavern. Faces, faces, faces, greens and grays intermingled, workmen all. In a moment of honesty, he had to admit that there was more variety and character in those faces than in the smooth soft countenance of the typical lower-bracket officer. These visages had been leaned down by a life-time of work, creased by squinting, dried by the hot wind of furnaces. He had gained considerable respect for manual skill; it took as much, in a way, to handle a lathe or a torch or a spraygun as to use slide rule and account book.

Only why should these complementary types be at War? They needed each other. Why couldn't they see the fact?

Several men filed onstage, accompanied by goons whose similar clothes suggested uniforms. Friday's mind wandered during the speech by the union's nominal president. The usual platitudes. He woke up when Wilson came to the rostrum.

He had to admit the Councillor was a personality. His voice was a superbly versatile instrument, rolling and roaring and sinking to a caress, drawing forth anger and determination and laughter. And the gross body, pacing back and forth, did not suggest fat, it was tigerishly graceful; a dynamo turned within the man. In spite of himself, Friday was caught up in the fascination.

Wilson deplored the riot, scolded his followers, exhorted them to forget their petty differences in the great cause of the voyage. He said he was recruiting "attendant auxiliaries" from green and gray alike, and mixing them up in squads, so that they could learn to know each other. They were fellow workers, they simply happened to have different jobs, they needed each other and the ship needed both.

"You *are* the ship! We've got to eat. We've got to have power, heat and light and air, tools, maintenance. *And nothing else.* Everybody else aboard is riding on your backs.

"Who keeps the ship moving? Who's pushing us to far Centauri? Not the officers' corps, not the Guildsmen, not the doctors and lawyers and teachers and policemen. Not even you, my friends. We reached terminal velocity eighty years ago. Old Man Inertia is carrying us to our far home. Don't let anybody claim credit for that, nobody but Almighty God.

"But we've got to eat on the way. We've got to have power to keep us alive, keep out the

cold and the dark and the vacuum. Once
landed, we'll still need all those things, we'll
have to start farms and machine shops. We
need *you*. You, green and gray, are the keel of
this ship, and don't you ever forget it!"

He went on, with a vast silence before him
and no eye in the chamber leaving his face.
The workers were one, they had to unite to see
the ship through, their feuds were a hangover
from the bad old days of unrestrained capitalism. He hinted broadly that certain
elements kept the pot boiling, kept the
workers divided among themselves lest they
discover their true strength and speak up for
their rights. He instilled the notion of cabals
directed against the crewmen—"who make
up more than six thousand people, out of
seven thousand!" and of plots to overthrow
the Council, establish all-out officer rule and
crush the workers underfoot.

"God, no!" cried Friday. He caught himself
and relapsed into his seat, half blind with
rage. His outburst had gone unnoticed in the
rising tide of muttered anger.

Trying to control himself, he analyzed the
speech as it went on. A wonderful piece of
demagoguery, yes. Nothing in it that could
really be called seditious—on the surface,
merely an exhortation to end rioting and
general lawlessness. No one was mentioned
by name except the Guilds, who didn't count
anyway. No overt suggestion of violence was
made. The Captain was always spoken of in
respectful tones, the hint being that he was

the unhappy prisoner of the plotters. A list of somewhat exaggerated grievances was given, but the ship's articles provided for freedom of speech and assembly. Oh, yes, very lawful, very dignified—and just what was needed to incite mutiny!

At the end, the cheering went on for a good quarter-hour. Friday clamped his teeth together, feeling ill with fury. When the racket had subsided, Wilson called for the customary question period.

Friday jumped up on his seat. "Yes," he shouted. "Yes, I have a question."

"By all means, brother Friday," said Wilson genially. So—he remembered.

"Are you preaching revolution," yelled Friday, "or are you lying because you can't help yourself?"

The silence was short and incredulous, then the howling began. Friday vaulted into the aisle and up onto the stage, too full of his rage to care what he was doing.

Wilson's voice boomed from the loud-speakers, slowly fighting down the tumult: "Brother Friday does not agree with me, it seems. He has a right to be heard. Gentlemen, gentlemen, quiet please!" When the booing had died down a little: "Now, sir, what do you wish to say? This is a free assembly of free men. Speak up."

"I say," said Friday, "that you are a liar and a mutineer. Your talk has been a stew of meaningless words, false accusations, and invitations to rebellion. Shall I go down the list?"

"By all means," smiled Wilson. "Brother Friday, you know, has a somewhat unusual background. I am sure his views are worth hearing."

The laughter was savage.

"I hardly know where to begin," said Friday.

"It is a little difficult, yes," grinned Wilson. The laughter hooted forth again, overwhelming him, knotting his tongue. He twisted the words out, slowly and awkwardly:

"Just for a start, then, Mr. Wilson, you said that the greens and grays together are almost the entire ship. Six out of seven thousand, you said. Anyone who's taken the trouble to read the latest census figures would know it's not true. There are about a thousand men working in all the branches of Engineering under officers, and about five hundred in the food section. There are about three hundred in public service of one sort or another—police, teachers, lawyers and judges, administrative clerks, and so on. Guildsmen and other independents together make up perhaps seven hundred. The entire officers' corps, *including their families*, add up to maybe five hundred. In short, out of some three thousand money-earning, working people aboard, greens and grays add up to half.

"I don't include the four thousand others—housewives, children and aged." With an essay at sarcasm: "Unless you want to enroll them in your goon squads too!" He turned to the assembly. "Fifteen hundred people in green and gray, to dictate to the other fifty-five hundred. Is that your precious democracy?"

"*Boo! Boo! Throw 'im out! Spy! Blackleg! Boo!*"

"You seem to be distorting my speech now," said Wilson mildly. "But go ahead, if it amuses you."

"God damn it, man, it's the ship I'm thinking about. I know there are plenty of abuses, I'm the victim of one myself—"

"Ah, yes, a pathetic fate," said Wilson lugubriously. "He was forced by incredibly cruel people to come down among us and earn his living!"

The shouting and the booing and cursing and laughing drove Friday off the stage. He hadn't a chance, he was beaten and routed; and he had been made ridiculous—which was much worse. He fled, sobbing in his throat, yelling at the silent corridors and damning the ship and the voyage and every stinking human aboard her. Then he found a bar and drank himself blind.

"I admire your courage," said William Johnson, "but I must admit your discretion leaves something to be desired. You should have known you had no chance against a professional politician."

"Now he tells me," said Friday ruefully.

"I hope it hasn't made things—difficult for you, Evan." There was an anxiety in Elena's voice which pleased him.

He shrugged. "I didn't lose too many friends. But I lost a lot of standing."

Oddly enough, his mind ran on, it had been Sam Carter who had defended him most stoutly in the barrack-room arguments, Sam who had beaten him up when he first arrived and now stood by him, though it meant damning Wilson. The fact was comforting, but puzzling. It was hard to realize that people just didn't fit into the next categories of tradition.

They were sitting in the Johnsons' apartment, a small bright place where he had been a frequent guest of late. He had fallen into the habit of dropping in almost "daily," for the merchant class had something to offer he had never looked to find on the lower levels, and something, besides, which was strange to the topdecks. The Johnsons and their associates were not the narrow-souled tradesmen their reputation among other classes insisted; they were, on the whole, people of quality and some little culture. If they had a major fault, he thought, it was a certain conservatism and timidity, a nostalgia for the "good old days" with which he could only partly sympathize. And they had their own tired clichés, meaningless words setting off automatic emotional responses—"free enterprise," "progressivism," "Radical"—but then, what class didn't?

He found himself increasingly aware of Elena. She was pleasant to look at and talk to; the other lower-deck women had seemed meretricious or merely dull. And at the same time she had an enterprising sincerity and an, at times, startlingly realistic world-view which would be hard to find in officers' women.

"And what do you expect to happen next?" asked Mrs. Johnson. The fact of Friday's being from topdeck earned him an automatic respect among Guildsmen, who still wanted leaders. Their own agitation was simply for justice to themselves, and Friday had to admit their cause seemed reasonable.

"Trouble. Open fighting—there've been brawls almost every watch between the goons of the Brotherhood and those of the officers. Maybe mutiny."

Johnson shuddered. He was bold enough in conversation, but physically timid. "I know," he said. "And the laborers have been making difficulties for private shopowners too. They've been smashing up bars, especially, when they're drunk."

"Want to socialize liquor, eh?" Elena's laugh was strangely merry. "Maybe we should call for a representative of the tavern-keepers on the Council."

"Only a representative of all tradesmen," said Johnson stiffy. To Friday: "We won't stand for it much longer. The younger Guildsmen are forming protective associations."

"Goons! Certainly *not!* Protect—"

"A goon by any other name would smell as sweet," said Elena. "Why not call them by their right name? If we have to fight, we'll need fighting units."

"Not much good without weapons and training," said Friday. "You have small machine shops here and there. You should start quietly making knives, knuckledusters, and so on, and exercise squads in their use. Wouldn't take long to equip every man."

"Why, you're speaking sedition!" whispered Johnson. "That's no better than Wilson."

Friday flung out of his chair and paced the floor. "Why not?" he said angrily. "It's not as if you meant aggression. The police can't be everywhere, and in any case they're under the control of whoever owns the Captain. At the moment, that happens to be an uneasy cabal of Engy and Astro officers, together with Wilson, who's nominally their associate and actually trying to get the power from them. If the officers win, you may expect to see a rigid caste system imposed on all the ship. If Wilson wins, you'll get a nominal communism which, if I've read any history at all, will rapidly become the same kind of dictatorship under different labels. Either way, the Guilds lose. You won't have a voice in affairs till you're strong enough to merit one."

"Evan, I thought you were an officer," said Elena, very softly. "I thought even now—"

"Of course I am! A ship has to have discipline and a hierarchy of authority, but that's precisely what we haven't got now. What I want to see is a strong captain with an officer corps made of the better existing elements—oh, such as my father, for instance, or Lieutenant Steinberg, or any of some hundred others. Most of the lower-echelon officers are decent and sincere men, Elena, they just haven't got any effective voice in affairs; they take orders from the Captain without regard to the fact that he takes *his* orders from two or three warring cliques. And the holes left in the corps could be filled competitively from the lower ranks."

"Ah—" Johnson cleared his throat shyly. "Pardon me, Evan, but wouldn't there be the same tendency as before for rank to become hereditary?"

"Naturally, superior people tend to have superior children," said Friday somewhat snobbishly. "But today, I admit, while there is still competitive examination for promotion, there is a certain favoritism in judging the results and few or no crewmen get the education needed to prepare for the tests." He clenched his fists. "God, what a lot of reform we need!"

Elena came over and took his hand. "You know more about the ship than anyone in the Guilds, Evan," she said. "Certainly your military knowledge is the best we can get. Will you be with us?"

He looked at her for a long while, "What have I been saying?" he whispered. "What have I been saying?"

"Good things, Evan."

"But—Bill, you're right. I have been talking violence." He smiled uncertainly. "I've been overworking my mouth lately, haven't I?"

"You won't help us—?"

"I don't know. God, I don't know! Taking the law into our own hands this way—it's contrary to the articles, it's contrary to everything I've ever believed."

"But we have to do it, Evan," she said urgently. "You advised it yourself, and you're right."

"Blast it, I'm still an Engy. I still have to live with my co-workers."

"You could quit your job and come live with us. The Guilds would pay you a good wage just to get their protective squads organized."

"So now I'm to become a paid goon!" he said bitterly.

"The time may come when the ship will need your goon squads."

"I don't know," he said dully. With sudden vehemence: "Let me think! I've been kicked into a level I don't understand, caught up in a business I don't approve. My father told me, before they sent me away, that I was still an officer. And yet—let me think it over, will you?"

"Of course, Evan," said Johnson.

He bade clumsy farewells and went out into the corridor and back toward his dwelling place, too preoccupied to notice the men who fell quietly in on either side of him. When one of them spoke, it was like a blow:

"This way, Friday."

"Eh? Huh?" He stared at them. Wilson's goons. "What the hell do you want?"

"We just want to take you to Mr. Wilson,

jo. He wants to see you. This way."

An elevator took them up to officer level. Actually, thought a dim corner of Friday's mind, the term should have been "down," since they were increasing centrifugal "gravity"; but the notion of the upper classes living "upward" was too ingrained for usage to change, even though on any one level "down" meant the direction of acceleration. Silly business.

The whole expedition was a cosmic joke.

He had not been in this territory for half a year, and it jarred him with remembrance. He stayed between his escorts, looking directly ahead, trying not to see the familiar people who went by. It was doubtful if any of them looked closely enough to recognize him.

Wilson's offices occupied a suite in the Administrative section, near the bows and just under the ship's skin. Her screens made that area as safe as any other, and the fact that the pilot room and hence the captain's quarters had to be directly in the bow on the axis of rotation—the only spot where there was an outside view except via telescreen— had dictated the placement of all officer areas nearby.

The inner office was a big one. Wilson had had it redecorated with murals which, in spite of their subjects—heroic laboring figures, for the most part—Friday had to admit were good. Indeed, these troubled decades had produced a lot of fine work.

He wrenched his attention to the man behind the great desk. Wilson sat easy and relaxed, puffing a king-sized cigar and studying some papers which he put aside when the newcomers entered. He rose courteously and smiled. "Please sit down, Mr. Friday," he said.

The two goons took up motionless posts by the door. Friday edged himself nervously into a chair.

"You know Lieutenant Farrell, of course," said Wilson.

Friday felt a shock at seeing the lean middle-aged man in officer's uniform seated at Wilson's right. Farrell—certainly he knew Farrell, the man had taught him basic science. Farrell had for years been a general assistant to Captain Gomez.

"I'm sorry to see you associated with this man, sir," he said numbly.

"Quite a few officers are," said Farrell gently. "After all, Mr. Wilson is a Councillor."

"Have a cigar, Mr. Friday," said Wilson.

"No, thanks. What did you want to see me about?"

"Oh—several things. I wanted to apologize for the somewhat unfortunate result of the union meeting. You had a right to be heard, and it is a shame that some of the men got a little rowdy."

You know damn well what made them that way, thought Friday.

"I liked your courage, even if it was misguided," said Wilson. "You're an able young man and honest. I'd like to have you on my side."

Friday wished he had accepted the cigar. It

would have been a cover for the silence that came from having no retort to make. *Another little political trick. I'll know better next time, if there is a next time.*

"You seem to think I'm some kind of monster," said Wilson. "Believe me, I have only the interests of the ship at heart. I think that we must be united in order to succeed in this voyage. But to achieve that union, we must have justice. You yourself, as a victim of the present system, ought to realize that."

"We need leadership first," said Friday slowly. "Good leadership, not political dictatorship."

"There is no intention of setting one up," said Farrell mildly. "Certainly you don't think that officers will be replaced by commissars! Would I be in this movement if that were the case? No, we simply want to replace the corrupt and the incompetent, and to install a socio-economic system adapted to the peculiar needs of the expedition."

"Nice words. But you're building up a private army, and you're planning mutiny."

"I could get angry at that charge," said Wilson. "Have I ever so much as suggested replacing the Captain? If the ship's articles are to be amended, it will be by due process of law."

"A rigged Council and a fixed election! Sure! Keep the Captain in his present job of figurehead!"

"Now it is you who are seditious. Look, Mr. Friday. I do believe you are innocent of the charges made against you, and I'd like to see you cleared and your rank restored. Promotion will be rapid for competent men, once things are running properly again. But these are tough times, and you can't expect me to take all that trouble for an enemy."

"So now you're trying to bribe me. Why, for all I know it was you who framed me in the first place."

Wilson's carefully learned manners dropped from him. It was a plain Engy who spoke, with more than a trace of anger: "Look, jo, d'you think you're so goddam important that it makes any difference what happens to you? You think I need you? I'm just trying to be fair, and give you a chance to get back where you were. You can be useful, sure, but you're not fixed to do any harm. Especially if you got fired from your job."

Friday stood up. "That's enough," he said. "Good-bye, Mr. Wilson."

"Have it your way, jo. If you change your mind, you can come back in a day or two. But don't be any later."

"I wish you would think it over," said Farrell.

"Good-bye!" Friday stormed out of the office.

He cooled off on the trip back. Gods, talk about burning bridges! He didn't belong anywhere now.

No—wait—the Guilds. He still didn't much like the thought of espousing their cause—but where else in all the universe could he go?

He took a certain malicious pleasure in telling off his boss when he quit. Then he drew his time, collected his few belongings, and went back to William Johnson's home.

The food trust was overthrown largely from within—a general strike of its underpaid workers, accompanied by violence—but that overthrow was instigated by leading Engineers as a means of overcoming their food-producing rivals. The Engineers wanted a return to the small private farms of the first years—*divide et impera*—but the upper ranks of Administration favored socializing the producing, packing, and distributing establishments, since they would then be under effective control of the small but efficient Admy bureaucracy. After a good deal of intriguing, socialism won, and the Engineers found themselves faced with a new rival as powerful as the old.

Two years later, Captain Petrie died. Both Engineering and Administration nominated a hand-picked successor, ignoring the rule that the first mate should take the office. This was a young man, Juan Gomez, associated with the Astrogation Department. Astro, being a small and exclusively officer group, lacked the strength and support of the contending overlords; but it had the law on its side, together with a surprising adroitness at playing its enemies off against each other. Gomez was named.

For a few years there was relative quiet,

except for clashes between various bully gangs hired by the overlords. The workers, green and gray, were increasingly restless, the younger generation of officers in all departments ever more arrogant and exclusive. In the forty-fifth year of the great voyage, open warfare broke out between the private forces of Engy and Admy over the exact extent of Admy jurisdiction—the latter had been using the ship's internal law, which it was supposed to administer, as a means of aggrandizing its leaders. It was not what Earth's bloody history would have considered a real war—the two sides lacked very effective weapons, and were small—but people were getting killed, property was damaged and vital services suspended. Astrogation rallied the police and neutral groups to suppress the fighting. The ship's articles were amended, the most important respect being the transfer of police power from Administration to the Captaincy—in effect, to Astro. Administration didn't like it, but the Engineers, on the old half-a-loaf principle, supported the measure. Astro began building up followers, money investments, and political connections.

Five years later the lower Engineering ranks, having failed to obtain satisfaction in any other way, resorted to violence. The revolt was suppressed, but concessions were made in a Captain's Court which few officers liked.

Six years after that, Duncan, chief of Ad-

minstration, attempted to seize the Captaincy
in a coup d'etat which was defeated with the
help of the Engineering bosses. Duncan and
his immediate followers suffered the usual
penalties of mutiny, but his power was left un-
broken and passed to his successor. This was
shown to be the work of Astro: in the sixty-
first year, Admy and Astro together swung
enough political power to break up officer
ownership of factories and socialize them,
and enough fighting strength to enforce the
decree.

Some fifteen years passed without too
much trouble as the ship adjusted to the new
order of things. All important facilities were
now under ship ownership and control,
tracing back ultimately to the Captain and his
Council. The old departmental divisions remained, but officers within them acted as
individuals and their combinations were
often across such party lines. Some wanted a
return to the former state of affairs, but most
were content to intrigue for control of this or
that department of ship life—ultimately, the
goal was to run the Council, from which all
authority stemmed. A combine made up largely of Astro officers held the balance of power,
but it was a constant battle of wits to
maintain it. In this period began the first
great outburst of characteristic ship forms of
art, literature, and music, new departures
which would have meant little to an Earthman but which answered a need born of space
and loneliness and the great overriding

purpose. In science, some first-rate work was done on deep-space astrophysics and the biological effects of cosmic radiation.

Meanwhile, however, the laboring classes demanded some voice in affairs. Unions were organized on a ship-wide basis and finally joined together in Wilson's Brotherhood. At this time, too, the remaining independents—craftsmen, artisans, tailors, tavern-keepers, personal-service people, private lawyers, and their kind, including no few scientists and artists of one sort or another—began organizing the Guilds for mutual protection and advancement; but they had no way to win an effective voice.

Labor, however, could and did act. The great strike of 2201 broke the time of peace. On the principle that certain services were essential to the lives of everyone, the Council tried to break the stroke, and for several days a running war was fought up and down the corridors of the ship. The union was finally suppressed, but it won what amounted to a victory, a representative on the Council. The old-line officers were outraged, but Wilson set to work at once making alliances with the younger and more liberal ones.

His official program was frankly communistic. The large fortunes and followings of the highest officers were to be broken up, all property except the purely personal was to belong to the ship, plants were to be governed by workers' councils. On the other hand, some kind of supreme heirarchy would still,

obviously, be needed; and no doubt many of
the ranking men who joined Wilson's cause
were animated by the thought of promotion.
There were also a certain percentage of
sincere idealists who were disgusted with the
intriguing and corruption of the ship's
government, the unseemly brawling, private
gangs, and the not yet overcome unfairness
of a caste system.

Besides Wilson's group, there were several
others in high places, with schemes of their
own. Certain men wanted to grab supreme
power for themselves; others wished a return
to this or that stage of previous ship's history,
say the good old days when the Engineers
virtually ran affairs, or to advance along
certain lines that seemed desirable to
them—such as, for instance, a frankly hereditary officer caste controlling all wealth and
authority.

Gomez still had the chairmanship of the
Council, the small but strong police force, and
a solid following among conservative
elements including the bulk of the officer's
corps and perhaps even a majority of the
common. And Astro had the Captain. One suspected that McMurtrie, chief of that department, had the final say in matters, though no
one outside of Astro knew for certain.

Only—how long could it continue? The ship
was ready for another explosion. How long
before it came?

Gods! thought Friday sick. *Gods, what a
history! What hell's broth of a history!*

He had about three weeks before the crisis broke, and had not thought he could go so long on as little sleep as he got.

There was first the matter of raising his troop. A call for volunteers at a special Guild meeting brought disappointing results. He and a few others had to go on personal recruiting tours, arguing and propagandizing and even applying certain subtle threats— social disapproval, boycotting, and whatever else could be hinted at obliquely enough not to antagonize. Some rather slippery sophistry got by at times, and Friday had to be careful to suppress his own uneasy doubts about his cause. The motto was always organization for defense, formation of a band which could help the regular police if they should need it, and he found it necessary to shout down the hotheads who had been his eagerest followers. He often had occasion to remember the ancient maxim that politics is the art of creating an equality of dissatisfaction.

He was helped by events. As the watches went by, disorder grew like a prairie fire. Hardly a "day" passed that the police were not called to stop a brawl between Wilson's gangs and the goons of other factions, or to halt the wrecking and plundering of some shop. They were bewildered and angry men who came to Friday, they wanted to fight somebody—it didn't much matter who.

"But what the glory is Wilson doing it for?" said Mrs. Johnson. "He's only hurting his own cause. He should be calming them down, or he'll turn all the ship against his people."

"That," said Friday with a bleak new insight, "is what he wants."

Officially, of course, the Councillor deplored such lawlessness and called on all workers to desist. But his language was weak; it only turned strong when he cited the grievances which had driven them to such measures. Friday buckled down to training his gang.

He had no military knowledge except vague impressions from books, but then neither did anyone else who mattered. Only the police were allowed firearms, and his conditioning was too deep for him to consider manufacturing them. It would hardly have been practicable anyway. But the tools of the artisans could make the nasty implements of infighting. And it occurred to him further that pikes, axes, and even short swords were valuable under ship conditions. However clumsily wielded, they were still formidable. He thought of bows too, but experiment showed him that more practice would be needed than his men had time or patience for.

He worked three shifts each day, drilling those who could attend any one of them. Practice with weapons, practice in working as groups, practice at rough-and-tumble—it was all he could do, and he more than half expected his motley squads to break and run if it ever came to action. He had about two hundred all told, shopkeepers, artisans, per-

sonal-service men, office workers, intellectu-
als of all stripes; a soldier's nightmare.

But after all, he consoled himself, it wasn't
really an army he was trying to organize. It
was an association of ordinary peaceable men
who had found it necessary to form their own
auxiliary police force. That was all. He hoped
to heaven that was all.

They used an empty storage space near
zero-gravity as their armory. You could do
weird and wonderful things at low-weight,
once you got the hang of it. He tried to be as
unobtrusive about his project as possible, and
especially to keep secret the fact of his most
lethal innovations. The police would most
likely confiscate things like those, if they
heard of them. All the rest of the ship needed
to know was that the Guildsmen had started a
protective association, and if the Brotherhood
wanted to make a huge joke of it, so much the
better.

Nevertheless, Friday was irrationally pleased when a few of his men got into a fight
with some greens in a bar and beat the devil
out of them.

He was catching an exhausted nap in Johnson's apartment when Elena woke him with
the news that the Brotherhood had mutinied.

"Oh, no!" he exclaimed. Sleep drained from
him like water from a broken cup as he got to
his feet.

"Yes," she said tonelessly. "The intercom
just announced a state of emergency, told all

crewfolk to get home and stay there and not to take part in any violence on pain of being considered mutineers—what else can it mean?"

He heard the brazen voice again, roaring out of the corridor loudspeaker, and nodded. "But I'd like to see it done," he said thinly. "The ship is six miles long and two miles in diameter. How does Wilson expect to take it over with a thousand men at best?"

"Seize the key points and the officers," she flared. "How else?"

"But the police—he can't hold anyplace against men with gas guns, firearms, grenades—"

"He must think he can! Are we going to sit here and do nothing?"

"Not much else we can do. That order to stay inside means us, too."

"Evan Friday, what have you been organizing the Guildsmen for?"

"Get on the visiphone," he said. "Call up everyone before somebody or other cuts off our communications. Tell them to stand by. But we can't go rushing out blindly."

She flushed him a smile. "That's more like it, Evan!"

He looked out the door into the hall. Men, women, children, were running each way, shouting, witless with panic—*This is revolution*, he thought. *You don't know what's happened, you don't know who's fighting or where the fighting is, you sit and wait and listen to the people going they don't know where.*

Presently Elena came to sit on the arm of his chair. "Where's father and mother?" she asked, and he saw the hard-held strength of her breaking as immediate pressure lifted. "They said they were going to visit Halvorson's; where are they—"

"I don't know,' he bit out. "They must have taken refuge with someone. We'll just have to wait here."

"I couldn't raise everybody," she said. "A lot of lines were jammed. But some of them said they'd pass the word along by messengers."

"Good! Good folk!" It was enormously heartening to know that some had remained brave and level-headed.

"I didn't even try to call headquarters," she said wryly. "But maybe we could offer the Captain our help."

"Let's see what happens first." Friday pounded his knee with a white-knuckled fist. "It's not that I'm scared to fight, Elena. In fact, I'm scared green to sit here and not fight. But we'd just blunder around, have no idea of where to go or what to do, probably get in the way of the police—"

The lights went out.

They sat for a moment in a blackness which was tangible. Elena choked a cry, and he heard the screaming of women out in the hall.

"Power cut off," he said unnecessarily,

trying to hold his voice steady. "Wait—hold still a minute." He strained his ears into the darkness and could not hear the muted endless hum of the ventilators. "Yeah. Dead off."

"Oh, Evan—if they hold the converters, they can threaten to destroy them—"

"Take more than they've got to do that, darling." The word came unconsciously, unnoticed by either of them. "But if they can hold off for a long enough time, they can make things awfully tough for the rest of the ship."

"It's—been tried before, hasn't it—?"

"Uh-huh, during the great strike. The police took the converters without difficulty and operated them till the trouble was over. So—if Wilson's tried it again, he must think he can hold the engine section against attack. Or maybe—maybe he doesn't expect an attack at all—"

"You mean the police are in his pay—no!"

"I don't know what I mean." Friday groped to his feet, and his only emotion was a rising chill of anger. "But it's time we found out. I'm going to get the men together."

They located a flashlight and went down the corridors toward the armory. It was utterly black save where their own beam wavered, a smothering blackness in which Friday thought he could hardly breathe. That was nonsense; the air wouldn't get foul for hours yet; but his heartbeat was frantic in his ears. People had retreated, the halls were almost empty—now and then another glow would bob out of the tunnel before them, a weirdly highlighted face. The elevators were dead; they used ringingly echoing companionways, down and down and down into the guts of the ship.

Silent ship, darkened ship; it was as if she were already dead, as if he and Elena were the last life aboard her, the last life in all the great hollow night between Sol and Centauri. Elena sobbed with relief when they came to the armory.

Friday had maintained a rotating watch there, sentries who challenged him in voices gone shrill with fear. Others were arriving, men and their families, the agreement being that in emergency this would be the rallying place. It was easily defensible, especially with the weapons stockpiled there.

Flashlights danced in the gloom, picking out faces and shimmering off metal, and the great sliding shadows flowed noiselessly around the thin beams. Friday shouted till the walls rang, calling the folk around him, seeking to allay the rising tide of hysteria.

"As soon as enough of us are here," he said, "we'll go out and see what we can do."

"The hell you say!" exploded a voice from the murk. "We'll stay here where we can defend ourselves!"

"Till the oxygen and the heat are gone? Would you rather choke and freeze?"

"They'll reach some agreement before then. Wilson can't let the whole ship die."

"They'll reach Wilson's kind of agreement,

if any. Something's happened so the police can't protect us any more. We'll have to act for ourselves."

"Go out and get killed in the dark? Not I, Mister!"

Friday had to resort to all the tactics of demagoguery—he was getting good at it, he thought—before the recalcitrants could be brought around. The agreement finally was that some men should stay to guard the women and children, while the rest would go out and—

And what? Friday did not dare admit that he had no idea. What, in all those miles of lightless tunnels and cave-like rooms, could they do?

There was an altercation at one of the doors. Friday went over to it and found a pair of pikemen thrusting back a shadowy and protesting group of men.

"Bunch of goddam workers want in," explained one of the guards.

Friday shone his torch into the vague mass and picked out the battered red face of Carter. "Sam! What the hell—"

"Fine way to treat us. We only want to join your bunch, Doc."

"Huh? I thought you were a Brotherhood man!"

"Yeah, but not a mutineer. I didn't think Old Tom'd ever try anything like this—just thought we'd roughhouse it a bit with the topdeck goons and holler for our rights. But God, Doc, his men got guns!"

"*What?*"

"Fact. Ain't too careful about using them, either. Me and some others that hadn't joined the goons were given a last chance to do it or get brigged—a goon squad come into the barracks and told us. But we got the jump on 'em, and here's my proof." The light glimmered off the pistol in Carter's fist. "We had a running fight to get down to low-weight, but others joined us on the way—some o' the boys who'd signed on as goons but didn't see mutiny, and others from here and there. They've took over the engine-section, Doc, and the gyros and the farms. There's men here with me who was on duty when the goons came in and kicked 'em out. Some of 'em had buddies who got shot for not moving fast enough. We wanna fight with you now, Doc!"

Numbly, Friday waved his sentries aside and let the workers file in. Gray and green, burly men with smoldering eyes, perhaps two score all told—a welcome addition, yes, but they were the heralds of evil tidings.

He let his watch sweep out another hour of darkness and restlessness and slowly rising temperature. Without regulation, the room was filled with animal heat of its occupants, the air was hot and foul. Later would come the cold.

Others straggled in, one by one or in small groups, Guildsmen and some more of the laboring class. But there was no further news, and presently the influx ceased. It was time to strike out.

A count-off showed that he had a little over
a hundred men ready to go. Go—where?

He decided to head for the upper levels.
There should be his best chance of getting information—there, too, was the nerve center of
the ship. If Wilson held her heart and lungs,
her brain might still be accessible.

They went out, a hundred men armed with
hand weapons of the oldest sort and a few
scattered guns, daunted by the night and their
loneliness. Silently, save for heavy breathing,
they streamed down the corridors and along
the companionways, only an occasional short
flash of light revealing them. Friday drew on
his memory of the ship's plan, which every
cadet was required to learn, to guide them
well away from the key points which Wilson
held. He didn't want more fighting than he
could avoid.

The ship was dark and still. Someone
whimpered behind him, a little animal sound
of fear.

They wound up the levels, feeling their
bodies grow heavier, feeling the sweat on
their skins and the bitter taste of panic in
their mouths. Once in awhile someone ran
before them, sandaled feet slapping down the
tunnel and fading back into the thick silence.

"God," whispered Carter. "What's happened to the ship?"

His voice was shaken, and Friday realized
that the same despair was rising in him. It
wouldn't take many hours of night and stillness and creeping chill before everyone

aboard capitulated, before the entire crew would be ready to assail anyone that still tried to resist. "Come on!" he said harshly.

They were in the upper levels when a flash gleamed far down the hall, someone nearing. Friday heard the sigh of tension behind him. If this was a mutineer gang and—

"Who goes?" The cry wavered in the dark. "Who is it?"

"Put up your hands," shouted Friday. The echoes ran down the length of the corridor, jeering at him.

"Come close."

It was a single man in Astro uniform. Friday recognized him—Ensign Vassily, secretary to Farrell. Farrell!

The gun was heavy in his fist. "What do you want?"

"Friday—Friday—" It was a sob. The flash-beam glistened off sweat and tears. "God, man, you're here! We've been looking—"

"Looking! What for? Aren't you with Wilson too?"

"Not now. The mutiny's got out of hand. Wilson has the police trapped, Farrell can't leave—he managed to send a few of us out, he knew of your gang—Friday, it's up to you, you've got to save the ship!"

"Out of hand— What the devil are you talking about?"

"Wilson was too smart." The boy's breath sobbed in his throat. "He didn't let any of his top chiefs in on his plans till it was too late. He—he started a riot down in Park Four, a big riot that brought out all the police force. Then his men—he'd gotten some firearms from a police officer that was with him, we didn't know he had anyone in the police— His men came with machine guns and flame throwers. They've got the force bottled up in the park—and meanwhile they've taken over the rest of the ship!"

So that was it, thought Friday. Simple! You lured all your enemies into one of the park sections and then mounted guard over the half-dozen exits. A few men with weapons and gas masks could keep a thousand besieged until cold and darkness and choking air forced them to surrender.

"Where do *you* fit in?" He shook Vassily till the teeth rattled in the ensign's jaws. "What do you mean, the mutiny's out of hand? Did you engineer it yourself?"

"Farrell—the Captain—I do not know, Friday, so help me God I don't know what it's all about!"

With a sudden terrible conviction: "Gomez and Farrell framed me, didn't they? They had me broken down to crewman!" When Vassily remained still, Friday cracked the pistol barrel against his head. "That's right, isn't it?"

"Uh—yes, no, I don't know—Friday, you've got to help us! We've been searching the ship for you, running down all the corridors with Wilson's men ready to shoot, you're the last one who can help!"

"Help?" Carter's laugh was bitter. "Spears

and axes against guns?"

"Most of Wilson's men don't have guns. He d-d-doesn't want 'em to get out of hand, I guess. Just the ones holding in the police, and holding the k-key points—"

Friday's mind began turning over with an abnormal speed and sureness. There wasn't time to be afraid, not now, not when all the ship was darkened. "That means the rest of the ship's weapons are still in the arsenal," he said rapidly. "I suppose Wilson's mounted guard over them?"

"I—I s-s-suppose so—"

Friday's memories riffled through the plans of the ship. The police quarters were near the bows, with the arsenal behind them, just under the ship's skin. Beyond that lay a boat blister, whose airlock offered an emergency exit—or entrance. Wilson's guards would be inside the ship, though, in front of the doors leading into the police area. He hoped!

There were other blisters along the length of the ship, holding the boats which would land when the *Pioneer* had taken up an orbit around a planet. And there were spacesuits stored at each one.

"This way!" he said.

It was strange walking on the outside. Eyes accustomed to a narrowness of walls swam with vertigo in naked space. Centrifugal force threw blood into the head, the heart began to beat wildly and the body refused to believe that it was not hanging downward. You had to be careful how you stepped—if both magnetic shoes were off the hull at once, you would be thrown into space, you could go spinning out and out forever into the dark between the stars.

Above your feet was the mighty curve of the ship, dimly gleaming metal tilted at a crazy angle against the sky, elliptical horizon enclosing all the life in more than a light-year of emptiness. It rang faintly under human footfalls, and the suit was thick with your heartbeat and breathing, but over that lay the elemental silence. It was a silence which sucked and smothered, the stupendous quiet of vacuum reaching farther than a man could think, and the tiny noises of life were unnaturally loud against it.

Below was the turning sky the constellations wheeling in fire and ice against a savage blackness, the chill glory of the Milky Way and the far green gleam of nebulae, hugeness, loneliness, and terror. The raw cold grandeur was like frost along the nerves; men felt sick and dizzy with the streaming of the stars.

Faint light glimmered off spacesuits and weapons as the troop made its slow way over the hull. About half the band had come out through four exits, and they clustered together for comfort against the hollow dark. Few words were spoken, but the harsh rasp of their breathing rattled in the helmet radios.

As they approached the bows, Friday could pick out the stabbing brilliance of Alpha Centauri—but Sol was lost somewhere in the thronging stars, nearly three light-years away. He found it hard to believe that the ship was rushing through space at fantastic velocity—no, it was motionless, it was lost forever between the stars.

And in the face of that immensity and that mission, he thought bitterly, men had nothing better to do than fight each other. With all the universe around them, they could not unite in a society which did not tear itself apart.

There was a certain cruel symbolism in the fact that it was Astrogation which had betrayed him— the men who steered between the worlds, dealing in rottenness and death. But after all, what else did those officers have to do? There were no planets between the suns, no orbital corrections to make—the department existed to keep alive the techniques and, meanwhile, to hold various posts connected with the general maintenance of the ship. And to stir up against each other men who should have been comrades—to break the innocent with lies, to provoke mutiny by injustice and intrigue, to infiltrate the revolts they themselves had created and control them for some senseless unknown purpose.

His jaws hurt with the clenching of his teeth. There was work to be done: enter the arsenal from outside, get the weapons, overcome the guards, then go on to park and fall on Wilson's men from behind so that the police could get out. Afterward it would be simple to clean up the rest of the mutineers; most likely they'd surrender at once when the police moved against them.

But after that—after that—!

Evan Friday walked slowly toward the door. It was strange to be back topside. After the noise and fury and belly-knotting terror of battle, after the lights had gone on again and folk had returned shakenly to resume life—of necessity, there had been amnesty for all rebels save the ringleaders—after the quite undeserved but pleasant adulation of gray and green and Guild, there had been a polite note requesting his attendance on the Captain, and he had donned his shabby best and gone. And that was all there was to it.

He felt no special emotion, it was drained from him and only a great quiet steadiness of purpose was left. It was no use hating anyone, they were all together in the ship and the ship was alone between the stars. But there was certain words he had to say.

The policeman at the door saluted him. "This way, please, sir," he said.

So now it's "sir" again. Do they think that can bribe me?

They went down a short hall and through an anteroom. The clerks looked up from their work with a vague apprehensiveness. Friday nodded to a man he had known a half a year ago—half a lifetime!—and at his escort's gesture went alone through the inner door.

There were three men sitting at the great table in the Captain's office—frail white-haired Gomez, lean gray Farrell, stocky dark

McMurtrie. They rose as he entered, and he stood with straining military stiffness. He couldn't help feeling naked without his uniform.

"How do you do, Ensign Friday." Gomez' old voice was hardly above a whisper. "Please be seated."

He found a chair and watched them out of cold eyes. "You are mistaken, sir," he answered. "I have no rank."

"Yes, you do, or rather you will as soon as that miscarriage of justice has been taken care of."

"Let us be plain with each other," said Friday flatly. "I know that you are responsible for my conviction. I also know that you and your associates engineered the mutiny, and that Wilson was only a force of which you made use. The casualties of the whole affair were some thirty killed and fifty wounded. If you had not summoned me here I would have come myself to charge you with murder."

There was pain in Gomez' slow reply: "And you would be perfectly justified. But perhaps the charge should be modified to manslaughter. We did not intend that there should be any death, and it weighs more heavily on us than you can imagine. But as you also know, the business got out of control, Wilson succeeded far beyond our expectations, and only your timely intervention saved us. Fortunately, the plan does not call for putting the ship into such danger again."

"I should hope not!" snapped Friday. "Before you go any further, perhaps I had better say that I left the traditional sealed envelope containing all I know with a friend. If I don't return soon, you may look for an unplanned uprising."

"Oh, you are in no danger," smiled Farrell. "It would hardly do for us to assault the next Captain."

"I—you—*what?*"

Numbly, Friday heard the voice continue: "In about five years, I imagine, you will be ready to succeed Captain Gomez."

He forced steadiness back, and there was a new anger in his reply: "Don't you think you can buy me that way, or any other. The whole structure of ship society is wrong. Our history has been one succession of bunglings, injustices, and catastrophes. I am here to call for a complete overhauling. And the first item will be to clean out the rotten blood-suckers who claim to be the leaders."

"Please, Mr. Friday," said McMurtrie, a little irritably. "Spare the emotional language till you've heard a bit more. For your information, every major wrong this expedition suffered has been created deliberately by the leaders—because they've really had no choice in the matter."

Friday glared at him. "You should know!" he spat. "You've run the whole dirty show, for twenty years this doddering fool has been your puppet, and—"

"I have not. The story goes, yes, that I am the power behind the throne. It's true that I've worked hard to keep things going. And I took the blame, because the Captain cannot afford it. He must have, if not the respect, at least the grudging acquiescence of the ship. But Captain Gomez is a very strong and skillful gentleman, and the decisive voice has always been his."

Friday shook his head. The maze of plot and counterplot, blinds and red herrings and interwoven cabals, was getting to be too much for him. "Why?" he asked dully. "What's the reason been? This is the greatest adventure man has ever faced, and now you say you've deliberately perverted it. If you aren't fiends and aren't madmen—*why?*"

"Let me start from the beginning," said Gomez.

He leaned back in his chair and half closed his eyes. "Psychology is a highly developed science these days," he said gently, "though for reasons which will become obvious it has been largely suppressed aboard ship. A potential leader is quietly given some years of intensive training in the field, for use later on—as you will be given it. And among the thousands of men who worked ten or twenty years on Earth planning this voyage, there were many psychologists. They could foresee events with more precision than I can convey to you; but I hope my bare words will be convincing.

"Consider the *Pioneer*. Once on her way, she

is a self-contained world. Everything we can possibly need to keep alive and comfortable is built into her. There is no weather, no disease, no crop failure, no earthquake, no outside invader, no new land to cultivate—nothing! A world potentially changeless! To be sure, for some twenty years the crew was still working on internal construction, but then that source of occupation and challenge was gone and there were still a hundred years or more of traveling left. A hundred years where a bare minimum of work would provide an excellent living for everyone.

"*What is the crew going to do in those hundred years?*"

For a moment Friday was taken aback at the question. The imbecile simplicity and the monstrous blindness of it held him dumb before he could answer: "Do? Why, God, man, the things that we have been doing, the worthwhile things that got accomplished in spite of all that went wrong. Science, music, the arts—"

McMurtrie gave him a scornful look. "What percentage of the population can keep amused that way?" he asked.

"Why—uh—ten per cent, maybe— But the rest— What's your psychology for, anyway? I've read books from Earth, I know there were primitive cultures where people were content to live perfectly uneventful, routine lives for thousands of years at a time. You could have created such a culture within the ship."

"And how fit would that culture be for the

hardships and dangers of Alpha Centauri?" demanded Farrell.

"It's a question of decadence," said Gomez persuasively. "If you read your history, you'll find that the decadent cultures, the ones without hope or enterprise or anything but puerile experimentation hiding a rockbound conservatism, have been those which lacked some great external purpose. They've been easier to live in, yes, until the decadence went so far that distintegration set in. The cultures which offered a man something to live for besides his own petty self—a crusade, a discovery, a dream of any kind, perhaps only the prospect of new land for settlement—have usually been violent, intolerant, unpleasant in one way or another, simply because everything else has been subordinated to the great purpose. I submit, as examples, Periclean Athens, Renaissance Italy, Elizabethan England, and nineteenth-century America, and ask you to compare them with, say, Imperial Rome or eighteenth-century Europe. You will also note that the greatest works of art and intellect were done in some of the most turbulent eras. As far as I can determine, the progress made aboard our ship has been rather because of than in spite of all our troubles."

"But damn it, man, we *have* a mission!" exploded Friday. "We're bound for far Centauri!"

"To be sure. That was the dream which sufficed the first generation. I don't say that unrest is a necessary component of non-decadence, in fact my whole argument has been grossly over-simplified. There was little strife in the beginning, because there was the great goal to dwarf men's petty differences.

"But what of the next generation, and the one after that, and the one after that, clear to Centauri? What was the goal to them but a vague thing in the background, an accepted part of everyday life—a thing which they would never see, or only see as very old people at best, a thing which had caused their lives to be spent in a cramped and sterile environment far from the green Earth? Don't you think there would have been a certain amount of subconscious resentment? And don't you think that the descendants of human stock deliberately chosen for energy, initiative, and general ability would have looked around for something worthwhile to do? And if nothing else is available, personal aggrandizement is a perfectly worthwhile goal."

"Couldn't—" Friday hesitated. The whole fiendish argument had a shattering conviction about it, and yet it seemed wrong and cruel. "Couldn't there have been a static culture for the in-between generations, and a revival of the dynamic sort in the generation that will reach Centauri young?"

"Now you're wallowing in wishful thinking," said McMurtrie. "Cultures have momentum. They don't change themselves overnight. Just tell me how you'd do all this, anyway."

Friday was silent.

"Believe me, all this was foreseen, and the solution adopted, while admittedly not very good, was the best available," said Farrell earnestly. "Conflict was inevitable. But if it could be controlled, properly directed, it could have great value, not only in keeping the dynamic society we will need at Centauri going, but also as a hard school for the unknown difficulties we will face then.

"Naturally, overt control is impossible. It has to be done indirectly—as far as possible, events simply have to take their natural course, with such men as know the secret and the techniques of psychology serving only as unnoticed guides.

"The initial setup was designed to cause a certain chain of development. The original small-scale private enterprises became monopolies in a very natural way, and their excesses provoked reactions, and so it has been throughout the history of the ship. Now and then things have gotten out of control, such as during the great strike, or the recent riots and mutiny, but by and large the plan has progressed in its ordained path—the path which, believe it or not, in the long run has produced the *minimum* possible unrest and conflict.

"Some men have striven for their own selfish ends, money or power—Wilson was one. We need their type for the plan, we offer it chances to develop—and at the same time, through the ultimate annihilating defeat of such men, we need the type out of our society. More men have responded in desirable ways.

They have demanded justice for themselves,
or for their class, or even—like yourself—for
classes not their own, for the ship as a whole.
Thus is born the type we ultimately want, the
hard-headed fighting visionaries."

"A hell of a way to get them," said Friday
disconsolately.

"The trouble with young idealists," said
Gomez dryly, "is that they expect all mankind
to live up to their own impossibly high
standards. When the human race obstinately
keeps on being human, these young men, instead of revising their goals downward to
something perhaps attainable, usually turn
sour on their whole species. But man isn't
such a bad race, Friday. Give him a little time
to evolve.

"As for you, I'd had my eye on you for a long
time. You were able, intelligent, stubborn in
your notions of right and wrong—all good
qualities for a skipper if I do say so myself.
You needed to be kicked out of a certain snob-
bishness and to learn practical politics. I
arranged for you to be thrown into a milieu
demanding such a development. If you'd
failed, you'd have been exonerated in time
and given some harmless sinecure. As it is,
you've responded so well that we think you're
the best choice for the next Captain—the one
who'll reach Centauri!"

Friday said nothing. There seemed nothing
to say.

"You'll go back to lower decks for a while
and lead the Guilds," resumed Gomez. "They

have a good claim now for a voice on the Council, having saved the ship and discovered their own strength. They'll get it, after some difficulty and agitation. You'll be cleared of the charges against you and restored to officer class with a higher rank, but remain Guild spokesman. In the course of time, the Guilds will build up power and ultimately join with Astro to oust the other factions from an effective voice. No violence, if it can be helped, but a restoration of mercantile economy. By then you should have learned enough psychology, practical and theoretical, to take over the Captaincy from me—which will, among other things, allay the old and perfectly correct suspicion that Astro has been quietly running the whole show all these years.

"Without going into detail on every planned event, there will be conditions aboard which, while actually quite tolerable, will contain enough social evil of one sort or another to call forth the best efforts of all men of good will, whether they know the great secret or not. Yes, we'll give them their causes to fight for! And in the end their striving will succeed; the just and harmonious order of this voyage's beginnings will be restored.

"It will be difficult, yes, it will take most of your lifespan. But the job should be completed by the time the ship is within four or five years of her goal. Then a satisfied and united humanity can begin making ready for the next great adventure."

His voice trailed off, and he looked down at his desk with a blindness that spoke the continuing thought: *The adventure I will never see.*

"Are you game?" asked McMurtrie. "Do you want the job?"

"I—I'll take it," whispered Friday. "I'll try."

Gomez did not look up. It was as if he were seeing through the desk and the floor and the walls and corridors and hull, out to the loneliness between the stars.

Yet emigration was no option for the billions left behind. The Humanist Manifesto shone like a beacon through the prevailing gloom. It promised personal fulfillment by restoring the simplicities of an imaginary past. ("What if there had been no Third World War?" was a popular premise for fantasies at this time.) The Humanists' anti-tech slogans ignited revolutionary ardor. Nevertheless, a fanatic's willingness to kill or be killed in the service of a cause cannot prove the rightness of that cause.

HOLMGANG

The most dangerous is not the outlawed murderer, who only slays men, but the rebellious philosopher; for he destroys worlds.

Darkness and the chill glitter of stars, Bo Jonsson crouched on a whirling speck of stone and waited for the man who was coming to kill him.

There was no horizon. The flying mountain on which he stood was too small. At his back rose a cliff of jagged rock, losing its own blackness in the loom of shadows; its teeth ate raggedly across the Milky Way. Before him, a tumbled igneous wilderness slanted crazily off, with one long thin crag sticking into the sky like a grotesque bow-sprit.

There was no sound except the thudding of

his own heart, the harsh rasp of his own
breath, locked inside the stinking metal skin
of his suit. Otherwise . . . no air, no heat, no
water or life or work of man, only a granite
nakedness spinning through space out beyond
Mars.

Stooping, awkward in the clumsy armor, he
put the transparent plastic of his helmet to
the ground. Its cold bit at him even through
the insulating material. He might be able to
hear the footsteps of his murderer conducted
through the ground.

Stillness answered him. He gulped a heavy
lungful of tainted air and rose. The other
might be miles away yet, or perhaps very
close, catfooting too softly to set up vibrations. A man could do that when gravity was
feeble enough.

The stars blazed with a cruel wintry
brilliance, over him, around him, light-years
to fall through emptiness before he reached
one. He had been alone among them before;
he had almost thought them friends. Sometimes, on a long watch, a man found himself
talking to Vega or Spica or dear old Beetle
Juice, murmuring what was in him as if the
remote sun could understand. But they didn't
care, he saw that now. To them, he did not
exist, and they would shine carelessly long
after he was gone into night.

He had never felt so alone as now, when
another man was on the asteroid with him,
hunting him down.

Bo Jonsson looked at the wrench in his

hand. It was long and massive, it would have been heavy on Earth, but it was hardly enough to unscrew the stars and reset the machinery of a universe gone awry. He smiled stiffly at the thought. He wanted to laugh too, but checked himself for fear he wouldn't be able to stop.

Let's face it, he told himself. *You're scared. You're scared sweatless.* He wondered if he had spoken it aloud.

There was plenty of room on the asteroid. At least two hundred square miles, probably more if you allowed for the rough surface. He could skulk around, hide . . . and suffocate when his tanked air gave out. He had to be a hunter, too, and track down the other man, before he died. And if he found his enemy, he would probably die anyway.

He looked about him. Nothing. No sound, no movement, nothing but the streaming of the constellations as the asteroid spun. Nothing had ever moved here, since the beginning of time when moltenness congealed into death. Not till men came and hunted each other.

Slowly he forced himself to move. The thrust of his foot sent him up, looping over the cliff to drift down like a dead leaf in Earth's October. Suit, equipment, and his own body, all together, weighed only a couple of pounds here. It was ghostly, this soundless progress over fields which had never known life. It was like being dead already.

Bo Jonsson's tongue was dry and thick in

his mouth. He wanted to find his enemy and give up, buy existence at whatever price it would command. But he couldn't do that. Even if the other man let him do it, which was doubtful, he couldn't. Johnny Malone was dead.

Maybe that was what had started it all—the death of Johnny Malone.

There are numerous reasons for basing on the Trojan asteroids, but the main one can be given in a single word: stability. They stay put in Jupiter's orbit, about sixty degrees ahead and behind, with only minor oscillations; spaceships need not waste fuel coming up to a body which has been perturbed a goodly distance from where it was supposed to be. The trailing group is the jumping-off place for trans-Jovian planets, the leading group for the inner worlds—that way, their own revolution about the sun gives the departing ship a welcome boost, while minimizing the effects of Jupiter's drag.

Moreover, being dense clusters, they have attracted swarms of miners, so that Achilles among the leaders and Patroclus in the trailers have a permanent boom town atmosphere. Even though a spaceship and equipment represent a large investment, this is one of the last strongholds of genuinely private enterprise; the prospector, the mine owner, the rockhound dreaming of the day when his stake is big enough for him to start out on his own—a race of individualists, rough and noisy and jealous, but living under iron rules of hospitality and rescue.

The Last Chance on Achilles has another name, which simply sticks an "r" in the official one; even for that planetoid, it is a rowdy bar where Guardsmen come in trios. But Johnny Malone liked it, and talked Bo Jonsson into going there for a final spree before checkoff and departure. "Nothing to compare," he insisted. "Every place else is getting too fantangling civilized, except Venus, and I don't enjoy Venus."

Johnny was from Luna City himself: a small, dark man with the quick nervous movements and clipped accent of that roaring commercial metropolis. He affected the latest styles, brilliant colors in the flowing tunic and slacks, a beret cocked on his sleek head. But somehow he didn't grate on Bo, they had been partners for several years now.

They pushed through a milling crowd at the bar, rockhounds who watched one of Archilles' three live ecdysiasts with hungry eyes, and by some miracle found an empty booth. Bo squeezed his bulk into one side of the cubicle while Johnny, squinting through a reeking smoke-haze, dialed drinks. Bo was larger and heavier than most spacemen—he'd never have gotten his certificate before the ion drive came in—and was usually content to let others talk while he listened. A placid blond giant, with amiable blue eyes in a battered brown face, he did not consider himself bright, and always wanted to learn.

Johnny gulped his drink and winced.

"Whiskey, they call it yet! Water, synthetic alcohol, and a dash of caramel they have the gall to label whiskey and charge for!"

"Everything's expensive here," said Bo mildly. "That's why so few rockhounds get rich. They make a lot of money, but they have to spend it just as fast to stay alive."

"Yeh . . . yeh . . . wish they'd spend some of it on us." Johnny grinned and fed the dispenser another coin. It muttered to itself and slid forth a tray with a glass. "C'mon, drink up, man. It's a long way home, and we've got to fortify ourselves for the trip. A bottle, a battle, and a wench is what I need. Most especially the wench, because I don't think the eminent Dr. McKittrick is gonna be interested in sociability, and it's close quarters aboard the Dog."

Bo kept on sipping slowly. "Johnny," he said, raising his voice to cut through the din, "you're an educated man, I never could figure out why you want to talk like a jumper."

"Because I am one at heart. Look, Bo, why don't you get over that inferiority complex of yours? A man can't run a spaceship without knowing more math and physical science than the average professor on Earth. So you had to work your way through the Academy and never had a chance to fan yourself with a lily white hand while somebody tootled Mozart through a horn. So what?" Johnny's head darted around, bird-like. "If we want some women we'd better make our reservations now."

"I don't, Johnny," said Bo. "I'll just nurse a

beer." It wasn't morals so much as fastidious-
ness; he'd wait till they hit Luna.

"Suit yourself. If you don't want to uphold
the honor of the Sirius Transportation Company—"

Bo chuckled. The Company consisted of (a)
the Sirius; (b) her crew, himself and Johnny;
(c) a warehouse, berth, and three other part
owners back in Luna City. Not exactly a
tramp ship, because you can't normally stop
in the middle of an interplanetary voyage and
head for somewhere else; but she went
wherever there was cargo or people to be
moved. Her margin of profit was not great in
spite of the charges, for a space trip is
expensive; but in a few more years they'd be
able to buy another ship or two, and eventually Fireball and Triplanetary would be getting
some competition. Even the public lines
might have to worry a little.

Johnny put away another couple of shots
and rose. Alcohol cost plenty, but it was also
more effective in low-gee. " 'Scuse me," he
said. "I see a target. Sure you don't want me
to ask if she has a friend?"

Bo shook his head and watched his partner
move off, swift in the puny gravity—the Last
Chance didn't centrifuge like some of the
tommicker places downtown. It was hard to
push through the crowd without weight to
help, but Johnny faded along and edged up to
the girl with his highest-powered smile. There
were several other men standing around her,
but Johnny had The Touch. He'd be bringing

one of its edges. On the other hand, he could just as well be bushwhacked from a ravine as he jumped over. And this route was the fastest for completing his search scheme.

The Great Bear slid into sight, down under the world as it turned. He had often stood on winter nights, back in Sweden, and seen its immense sprawl across the weird flicker of aurora; but even then he wanted the space-man's experience of seeing it from above. Well, now he had his wish, and much good it had done him.

He went over the edge of the cliff, cautious-ly, for it wouldn't take much of an impetus to throw him off this rock entirely. Then his helpless and soon frozen body would be just another meteor for the next million years. The vague downward sensation of gravity shifted insanely as he moved; he had the feeling that the world was tilting around him. Now it was the precipice which was a scarred black plain underfoot, reaching to a saw-toothed bluff at its farther edge.

He moved with flat low-gee bounds. Besides the danger of springing off the asteroid entirely, there was its low acceleration to keep a man near the ground; jump up a few feet and it would take you a while to fall back. It was utterly silent around him. He had never thought there could be so much stillness.

He was halfway across when the bullet came. He saw no flash, heard no crack, but suddenly the fissured land before him explod-ed in a soundless shower of chips. The bullet

ricocheted flatly, heading off for outer space.
No meteor gravel, that!

Bo stood unmoving an instant, fighting the
impulse to leap away. He was a spaceman, not
a rockhound; he wasn't used to this environment, and if he jumped high he could be
riddled as he fell slowly down again. Sweat
was cold on his body. He squinted, trying to
see where the shot had come from.

Suddenly he was zigzagging off across the
plain toward the nearest edge. Another bullet
pocked the ground near him. The sun rose, a
tiny heatless dazzle blinding in his eyes.

Fire crashed at his back. Thunder and darkness exploded before him. He lurched
forward, driven by the impact. Something
was roaring, echoes clamorous in his helmet.
He grew dimly aware that it was himself.
Then he was falling, whirling down into the
black between the stars.

There was a knife in his back, it was white-
hot and twisting between the ribs. He
stumbled over the edge of the plain and fell,
waking when his armor bounced a little
against stone.

Breath rattled in his throat as he turned his
head. There was a white plume standing over
his shoulder, air streaming out through the
hole and freezing its moisture. The knife in
him was not hot, it was cold with an ultimate
cold.

Around him, world and stars rippled as if
seen through heat, through fever. He hung on
the edge of creation by his fingertips, while

chaos shouted beneath.

Theoretically, one man can run a spaceship, but in practice two or three are required for non-military craft. This is not only an emergency reserve, but a preventive of emergencies, for one man alone might get too tired at the critical moments. Bo knew he wouldn't be allowed to leave Archilles without a certified partner, and unemployed spacemen available for immediate hiring are found once in a Venusian snowfall.

Bo didn't care the first day. He had taken Johnny out to Helmet Hill and laid him in the barren ground to wait, unchanging now, till Judgment Day. He felt empty then, drained of grief and hope alike, his main thought a dull dread of having to tell Johnny's father when he reached Luna. He was too slow and clumsy with words; his comforting hand would only break the old man's back. Old Malone had given six sons to space, Johnny was the last; from Saturn to the sun, his blood was strewn for nothing.

It hardly seemed to matter that the Guards office reported itself unable to find the murderer. A single Venusian should have been easy to trace on Achilles, but he seemed to have vanished completely.

Bo returned to the transient quarters and dialed Valeria McKittrick. She looked impatiently at him out of the screen. "Well," she said, "what's the matter? I thought we were blasting today."

"Hadn't you heard?" asked Bo. He found it hard to believe she could be ignorant, here where everybody's life was known to everybody else. "Johnny's dead. We can't leave."

"Oh . . . I'm sorry. He was such a nice little man—I've been in the lab all the time, packing my things, and didn't know." A frown crossed her clear brow. "But you've got to get me back. I've engaged passage to Luna with you."

"Your ticket will be refunded, of course," said Bo heavily. "But you aren't certified, and the *Sirius* is licensed for no less than two operators."

"Well . . . damn! There won't be another berth for weeks, and I've *got* to get home. Can't you find somebody?"

Bo shrugged, not caring much, "I'll circulate an ad if you want, but—"

"Do so, please. Let me know." She switched off.

Bo sat for a moment thinking about her. Valeria McKittrick was worth considering. She wasn't beautiful in any conventional sense but she was tall and well built; there were good lines in the strong high boned face, and her hair was a cataract of spectacular red. And brains, too . . . you didn't get to be a physicist with the Union's radiation labs for nothing. He knew she was still young, and that she had been on Achilles for about a year working on some special project and was now ready to go home.

She was human enough, had been to most of the officers' parties and danced and laughed

and flirted mildly, but even the dullest
rockhound gossip knew she was too lost in
her work to do more. Out here a woman was
rare, and a virtuous woman unheard-of; as a
result, unknown to herself, Dr. McKittrick's
fame had spread through more thousands of
people and millions of miles than her
professional achievements were ever likely to
reach.

Since coming here, on commission from the
Lunar lab, to bring her home, Bo Jonsson had
given her an occasional wistful thought. He
liked intelligent women, and he was getting
tired of rootlessness. But of course it would
be a catastrophe if he fell in love with her because she wouldn't look twice at a big dumb
slob like him. He had sweated out a couple of
similar affairs in the past and didn't want to
go through another.

He placed his ad on the radinews circuit
and then went out to get drunk. It was all he
could do for Johnny now, drink him a final
wassail. Already his friend was cold under the
stars. In the course of the evening he found
himself weeping.

He woke up many hours later. Achilles ran
on Earth time but did not rotate on it;
officially, it was late at night, actually the
shrunken sun was high over the domes. The
man in the upper bunk said there was a
message for him; he was to call one Einar
Lundgard at the Comet Hotel soonest.

The Comet! Anyone who could afford a
room to himself here, rather than a kip in the

public barracks, was well fueled. Bo swallowed a tablet and made his way to the visi and dialed. The robo-clerk summoned Lundgard down to the desk.

It was a lean, muscular face under close cropped brown hair which appeared in the screen. Lundgard was a tall and supple man, somehow neat even without clothes. "Jonsson," said Bo. "Sorry to get you up, but I understood—"

"Oh, yes. Are you looking for a spaceman? I heard your ad and I'm available."

Bo felt his mouth gape open. "Huh? I never thought—"

"We're both lucky, I guess." Lundgard chuckled. His English had only the slightest trace of accent, less than Bo's. "I thought I was stashed here too for the next several months."

"How does a qualified spaceman happen to be marooned?"

"I'm with Fireball, was on the Drake—heard of what happened to her?"

Bo nodded, for every spaceman knows exactly what every spaceship is doing at any given time. The *Drake* had come to Achilles to pick up a cargo of refined thorium for Earth; while she lay in orbit, she had somehow lost a few hundred pounds of reaction-mass water from a cracked gasket. Why the accident should have occurred, nobody knew... spacemen were not careless about inspections, and what reason would anyone have for sabotage? The event had taken place about a

month ago, when the *Sirius* was already
enroute here; Bo had heard of it in the course
of shop talk.

"I thougth she went back anyway," he said.
Lundgard nodded. "She did. It was the
usual question of economics. You know what
refined fuel water costs in the Belt; also, the
delay while we got it would have carried
Earth and Achilles past optimum position,
which'd make the trip home that much more
expensive. Since we had one more man
aboard than really required, it was cheaper to
leave him behind; the difference in mass
would make up for the fuel loss. I volunteered, even sugested the idea, because . . .
well, it happened during my watch, and even
if nobody blamed me I couldn't help feeling
guilty."

Bo understood that kind of loyalty. You
couldn't travel space without men who had it.

"The Company beamed a message: I'd stay
here till their schedule permitted an under-
manned ship to come by, but that wouldn't be
for maybe months," went on Lundgard. "I
can't see sitting on this lump that long
without so much as a chance at planetfall
bonus. If you'll take me on, I'm sure the
Company will agree; I'll get a message to them
on the beam right away."

"Take us a while to get back," warned Bo.
"We're going to stop off at another asteroid to
pick up some automatic equipment, and won't
go into hyperbolic orbit till after that. About
six weeks from here to Earth, all told."

"Against six months here?" Lundgard laughed; it emphasized the bright charm of his manner. "Sunblaze, I'll work for free."

"No need to. Bring your papers over tomorrow, huh?"

The certificate and record were perfectly in order, showing Einar Lundgard to be a Space-tech 1/cl with eight years' experience, qualified as engineer, astronaut, pilot, and any other of the thousand professions which have run into one. They registered articles and shook hands on it. "Call me Bo. It really is my name . . . Swedish."

"Another squarehead, eh?" grinned Lundgard. "I'm from South America myself."

"Notice a year's gap here," said Bo, pointing to the service record. "On Venus."

"Oh, yes. I had some fool idea about settling but soon learned better. I tried to farm, but when you have to carve your own land out of howling desert— Well, let's start some math, shall we?"

They were lucky, not having to wait their turn at the station computer; no other ship was leaving immediately. They fed it the data and requirements, and got back columns of numbers: fuel requirements, acceleration times, orbital elements. The figures always had to be modified, no trip ever turned out just as predicted, but that could be done when needed with a slipstick and the little ship's calculator.

Bo went at his share of the job doggedly, checking and re-checking before giving the problem to the machine; Lundgard breezed through it and spent his time while waiting for Bo in swapping dirty limericks with the tech. He had some good ones.

The *Sirius* was loaded, inspected, and cleared. A "scooter" brought her three passengers up to her orbit, they embarked, settled down, and waited. At the proper time, acceleration jammed them back in a thunder of rockets.

Bo relaxed against the thrust, thinking of Achilles falling away behind them. "So long," he whispered. "So long, Johnny."

III

In another minute, he would be knotted and screaming from the bends, and a couple of minutes later he would be dead.

Bo clamped his teeth together, as if he would grip consciousness in his jaws. His hands felt cold and heavy, the hands of a stranger, as he fumbled for the supply pouch It seemed to recede from him, down a hollow infinite corridor where echoes talked in a language he did not know.

"Damn," he gasped. "Damn, damn, damn, damn, damn."

He got the pouch open somehow. The stars wheeled around him. There were stars buzzing in his head, like cold white fireflies, buzzing and buzzing in the enormous ringing emptiness of his skull. Pain jagged through him, he felt his eardrums popping as pressure dropped.

The plastic patch stuck to his metal gaunt-

let. He peeled it off, trying not to howl with
the fury ripping in his nerves. His body was
slow, inert, a thing to fight. There was no
more feeling in his back, was he dead already?

Redness flamed before his eyes, red like
Valeria's hair blowing across the stars. It was
sheer reflex which brought his arms around
to slap the patch over the hole in his suit. The
adhesive gripped, drying fast in the sucking
vacuum. The patch bellied out from internal
air pressure, straining to break loose and kill
him.

Bo's mind wavered back toward life. He
opened the valves wide on his tanks, and his
thermostatic capacitors pumped heat back
into him. For a long time he lay there, only
lungs and heart had motion. His throat felt
withered and flayed, but the rasp of air
through it was like being born again.

Born, spewed out of an iron womb into a
hollowness of stars and cold, to lie on naked
rock while the enemy hunted him. Bo shuddered and wanted to scream again.

Slowly he groped back toward awareness.
His frostbitten back tingled as it warmed up
again, soon it would be afire. He could feel a
hot trickling of blood, but it was along his
right side. The bullet must have spent most of
its force punching through the armor,
caromed off the inside, scratched his ribs, and
fallen dead. Next time he probably wouldn't
be so lucky. A magnetic-driven .30 slug would
go right through a helmet, splashing brains as
it passed.

He turned his head, feeling a great weariness, and looked at the gauges. This had cost him a lot of air. There was only about three hours worth left. Lundgard could kill him simply by waiting.

It would be easy to die. He lay on his back, staring up at the stars and the spilling cloudy glory of the Milky Way. A warmth was creeping back into numbed hands and feet; soon he would be warm all over, and sleepy. His eyelids felt heavy, strange that they should be so heavy on an asteroid.

He wanted terribly to sleep.

There wasn't much room in the *Sirius*, the only privacy was gained by drawing curtains across your bunk. Men without psych training could get to hate each other on a voyage. Bo wondered if he would reach Luna hating Einar Lundgard.

The man was competent, a willing worker, tempering his cheerfulness with tact, always immaculate in the heat blue and white of the Fireball Line which made Bo feel doubly sloppy in his own old gray coverall. He was a fine conversationalist with an enormous stock of reminiscence and ideas, witty above a certain passion of belief. It seemed as if he and Valeria were always talking, animated voices like a sound of life over the mechanical ship-murmurs, while Bo sat dumbly in a corner wishing he could think of something to say.

The trouble was, in spite of all his efforts, he was doing a cometary dive into another bad case of one-sided love. When she spoke in that husky voice of hers, gray gleam of eyes under hair that floated flaming in nullgee, the beauty he saw in her was like pain. And she was always around. It couldn't be helped. Once they had gone into free fall he could only polish so much metal and tinker with so many appliances; after that they were crowded together in a long waiting.

—"And why were you all alone in the Belt?" asked Lundgard. "In spite of all the romantic stories about the wild free life of the rock-hound, it's the dullest place in the System."

"Not to me," she smiled. "I was working. There were experiments to be done, factors to be measured, away from solar radiation. There are always ions around inside the orbit of Mars to jumble up a delicate apparatus."

Bo sat quiet, trying to keep his eyes off her. She looked good in shorts and half-cape. Too good.

"It's something to do with power beaming, isn't it?" Lundgard's handsome face creased in a frown. "Afraid I don't quite understand. They've been beaming power on the planets for a long time now."

"So they have," she nodded. "What we're after is an interplanetary power beam. And we've got it." She gestured to the baggage rack and a thick trunk full of papers she had put there. "That's it. The basic circuits, factors and constants. Any competent engineer could draw up a design from them."

"Hmmm . . . precision work, eh?"

"Obviously! It was hard enough to do on, say, Earth—you need a *really* tight beam in just the right frequencies, a feedback signal to direct each beam at the desired outlet, relay stations—oh, yes, it was a ten-year research project before they could even think about building. An interplanetary beam has all those problems plus a number of its own. You have to get the dispersion down to a figure so low it hardly seems possible. You can't use feedback because of the time lag, so the beams have to be aimed *exactly* right—and the planets are always moving, at miles per second. An error of one degree would throw your beam almost two million miles off in crossing one A. U. And besides being so precise, the beam has to carry a begawatt at least to be worth the trouble. The problem looked insoluble till someone in the Order of Planetary Engineers came up with an idea for a trick control circuit hooked into a special computer. My lab's been working together with the Order on it, and I was making certain final determinations for them. It's finished now . . . twelve years of work and we're done." She laughed. "Except for building the stations and getting the bugs out!"

Lundgard cocked an oddly sardonic brow. "And what do you hope for from it?" he asked. "What have the psychotechs decided to do with this thing?"

"Isn't it obvious?" she cried. "Power! Nuclear fuel is getting scarcer every day, and civilization is finished if we can't find another energy source. The sun is pouring out more than we'll ever need, but sheer distance dilutes it below a useful level by the time it gets to Venus.

"We'll build stations on the hot side of Mercury. Orbital stations can relay. We can get the beams as far out as Mars without too much dispersion. It'll bring down the rising price of atomic energy, which is making all other prices rise, and stretch our supply of fissionables for centuries more. No more fuel worries, no more Martians freezing to death because a converter fails, no more clad feuds on Venus starting over uranium beds—" The excited flush on her cheeks was lovely to look at.

Lundgard shook his head. There was a sadness in his smile. "You're a true child of the New Englightenment," he said. "Reason will solve everything. Science will find a cure for all our ills. Give man a cheap energy source and leave him forever happy. It won't work, you know."

Something like anger crossed her eyes. "What are you?" she asked. "A Humanist?"

"Yes," said Lundgard quietly.

Bo started. He'd known about the antipsychotechnic movement which was growing on Earth, seen a few of its adherents, but—

"I never thought a spaceman would be a Humanist," he stammered.

Lundgard shrugged wryly. "Don't be afraid, I don't eat babies. I don't even get hysterics in an argument. All I've done is use the scientific method, observing the world without pre-conceptions, and learned by it that the scientific method doesn't have all the answers."

"Instead," said Valeria scornfully, "we should all go back to church and pray for what we want rather than working for it."

"Not at all," said Lundgard mildly. "The New Englightenment is—or was, because it's dying—a very natural state of mind. Here Earth had come out of the World Wars, racked and ruined, starving and chaotic, and all because of unbridled ideology. So the physical scientists produced goods and machines and conquered the planets; the biologists found new food sources and new cures for disease; the psychotechs built up their knowledge to a point where the socio-economic unity could really be planned and the plan worked. Man was unified, war had sunken to an occasional small 'police action,' people were eating and had comfort and security—all through applied, working science. Naturally they came to believe reason would solve their remaining problems. But this faith in reason was itself an emotional reaction from the preceding age of un-reason.

"Well, we've had a century of enlighten-ment now, and it has created its own troubles which it cannot solve. No age can handle the difficulties it raises for itself; that's left to the next era. There are practical problems arising, and no matter how desperately the psychotechs work they aren't succeeding with them."

"What problems?" asked Bo, feeling a little bewildered.

"Man, don't you ever see a newscast?" challenged Lundgard. The Second Industrial Revolution, millions of people thrown out of work by the new automata. They aren't going hungry, but they are displaced and bitter. The economic center of Earth is shifting to Asia, the poitical power with it, and hundreds of millions of Asians are skeptical aboard this antiseptic New Order the West has been bringing them: cultural resistance, and not all the psychotechnic propaganda in the System can shake it off. The men of Mars, Venus, the Belt, the Jovian moons are developing their own civilizations—inevitably, in alien environments; their own ways of living and thinking, which just don't fit into the neat scheme of an Earth-dominated Solar Union. The psychotechs themselves are being driven to oligarchic, unconstitutional acts; they have no choice, but it's making them enemies.

"And then there's the normal human energy and drive. Man can only be safe and sane and secure for so long, then he reacts. This New Enlightenment is really a decadent age, a period where an exhausted civilization has been resting under a holy status quo. It can't last. Man always wants something new."

"You Humanists talk a lot about 'man's right to variability,' " said Valeria. "If you really carry off that revolution your writings advocate you'll just trade one power group for another—and more fanatic, less lawful, than the present one."

"Not necessarily," said Lundgard. "After all, the Union will probably break up. It can't last forever. All we want to do is hasten the day because we feel that it's outlived its usefulness."

Bo shook his head. "I can't see it," he said heavily. "I just can't see it. All those people—the Lunarites, the violent clansmen on Venus, the stiff correct Martians, the asteroid rockhounds, even those mysterious Jovians—they all came from Earth. It was Earth's help that made their planets habitable. We're all men, all one race."

"A fiction," said Lundgard. "The human race is a fiction. There are only small groups with their own conflicting interests."

"And if those conflicts are allowed to break into war—" said Valeria. "Do you know what a lithium bomb can do?"

There was a reckless gleam in Lundgard's eyes. "If a period of interplanetary wars is necessary, let's get it over with," he answered. "Enough men will survive to build something better. This age has gotten stale. It's petrifying. There have been plenty of shake-ups in history—the fall of Rome, the Reformation, the Napoleonic Wars, the World Wars. It's been man's way of progressing."

"I don't know about all those," said Bo slowly. "I just know I wouldn't want to live through such a time."

"You're soft," said Lundgard. "Down underneath you're soft." He laughed disarmingly. "Pardon me. I didn't mean anything personal. I'll never convince you and you'll never convince me, so let's keep it friendly. I hope you'll have some free time on Luna, Valeria. I know a little grill where they serve the best synthosteaks in the System."

"All right," she smiled. "It's a date."

Bo mumbled some excuse and went aft. He was still calling her Dr. McKittrick.

IV

You can't just lie here and let him come kill you.

There was a picture behind his eyes; he didn't know if it was a dream or a long buried memory. He stood under an aspen which quivered and rustled as if it laughed to itself softly, softly, when the wind embraced it. And the wind was blowing up a red granite slope, wild and salt from the Sound, and there were towering clouds lifting over Denmark to the west. The sunlight rained and streamed through aspen leaves, broken, shaken, falling in spatters against the earth, and he, Bo Jonsson, laughed with the wind and the tree and the far watery glitter of the Sound.

He opened his eyes, wearily, like an old man. Orion was marching past, and there was a blaze on crags five miles off which told of the rising sun. The asteroid spun swiftly; he had been here for many of its days now, and each day burdened him like a year.

Got to get out of here, he knew.

He sat up, pain tearing along his furrowed breast. Somehow he had kept the wrench with him, he stared at it in a dull wonder.

Where to go, where to hide, what to do?

Thirst nagged him. Slowly he uncoiled the tube which led from the electrically heated canteen welded to his suit, screwed its end into the helmet nipple, thumbed down the clamp which closed it, and sucked hard. It helped a little.

He dragged himself to his feet and stood swaying, only the near-weightlessness kept him erect. Turning his head in its transparent cage, he saw the sun rise, and bright spots danced before him when he looked away.

His vision cleared, but for a moment he thought the shadow lifting over a nearby ridge was a wisp of unconsciousness. Then he made out the bulky black-painted edge of it, gigantic against the Milky Way, and it was Lundgard, moving unhurriedly up to kill him.

A dark laughter was in his radio earphones. "Take it easy, Bo. I'll be there in a minute."

He backed away, his heart a sudden thunder, looking for a place to hide. Down! Get down and don't stand where he can see you! He crouched as much as the armor would allow and broke into a bounding run.

A slug spat broken stone near his feet. The powdery dust hung for minutes before settling. Breath rattled in his throat. He saw the lip of a meteoric crater and dove.

Crouching there, he heard Lundgard's voice again: "You're somewhere near. Why not come out and finish it now?"

The radio was non-directional, so he snapped back: "A gun against a monkey wrench?"

Lundgard's coolness broke a little; there was almost a puzzled note: "I hate to do this. Why can't you be reasonable? I don't want to kill you."

"The trouble," said Bo harshly, "is that I want to kill you."

"Behold the man of the New Englightenment!" Bo could imagine Lundgard's grin. It would be tight, and there would be sweat on the lean face, but the amusement was genuine. Didn't you believe sweet reasonableness could solve everything? This is only the beginning, Bo, just a small preliminary hint that the age of reason is dying. I've already converted you to my way of thinking, by the very fact you're fighting me. Why not admit it?"

Bo shook his head—futile gesture, looked in darkness where he lay. There was a frosty blaze of stars when he looked up.

It was more than himself and Johnny Malone, more even than the principle of the thing and the catastrophe to all men which Lundgard's victory meant. There was something deep and primitive which would not let him surrender, even in the teeth of annihilation. Valeria's image swayed before him.

Lundgard was moving around, peering over the shadowy tumble of blackened rock in search of any trace. There was a magnetic rifle in his hands. Bo strained his helmet to the crater floor, trying to hear ground vibrations, but there was nothing. He didn't know where Lundgard was, only that he was very near.

Blindly, he bunched his legs and sprang out of the pit.

They found the asteroid where Valeria had left her recording instruments. It was a tiny drifting fragment of a world which had never been born, turning endlessly between the constellations; the *Sirius* moored fast with grapples, and Valeria donned a spacesuit and went out to get her apparatus. Lundgard accompanied her. As there was only work for two, Bo stayed behind.

He slumped for a while in the pilot chair, letting his mind pace through a circle of futility. Valeria, Valeria—O strong and fair and never to be forgotten, would he ever see her again after they made Luna?

This won't do, he told himself dully. *I should at least keep busy. Thank God for work.*

He wasn't much of a thinker, he knew that, but he had cleverness in his hands. It was satisfying to watch a machine come right under his tools. Working, he could see the falseness of Lundgard's philosophy. The man could quote history all he wanted; weave a glittering circle of logic around Bo's awkward brain, but it didn't change facts. Maybe this century was headed for trouble; maybe psychotechnic government was only another human self-limitation and should be changed for something else; nevertheless, the truth remained that most men were workers who wished no more than peace in which to create as best they could. All the high ideals in the universe weren't worth breaking the Union for and smashing the work of human hands in a single burst of annihilating flame.

I can feel it, down inside me. But why can't I say it?

He got up and went over to the baggage rack, remembering that Lundgard had dozens of book-reels along and that reading would help him not to think about what he could never have.

On a planet Bo would not have dreamed of helping himself without asking first. But custom is different in space, where there is no privacy and men must be a unit if they are to survive. He was faintly surprised to see that Lundgard's personal suitcase was locked; but it would be hours, probably, before the owner got back: dismantling a recorder setup took time. A long time, in which to talk and laugh with Valeria. In the chill spatial radiance, her hair would be like frosty fire.

Casually, Bo stooped across to Lundgard's sack-hammock and took his key ring off the hook. He opened the suitcase and lifted out some of the reels in search of a promising title.

Underneath them were neatly folded clothes, Fireball uniforms and fancy dress pajamas. A tartan edge stuck out from below, and Bo lifted a coat to see what clan that was. Probably a souvenir of Lundgard's Venusian stay—

Next to the kilt was a box which he recognized. L-masks came in such boxes.

How the idea came to him, he did not know. He stood there for minutes, looking at the box without seeing it. The ship was very quiet around him. He had a sudden feeling that the walls were closing in.

When he opened the box, his hands shook, and there was sweat trickling along his ribs.

The mask was of the latest type, meant to fit over the head, snug around the cheeks and mouth and jaws. It was like a second skin, reflecting expression, not to be told from a real face. Bo saw the craggy nose and the shock of dark hair, limp now, but—

Suddenly he was back on Achilles, with riot roaring around him and Johnny Malone's body in his arms.

No wonder they never found that Venusian. There never was any.

Bo felt a dim shock when he looked at the chronometer. Only five minutes had gone by while he stood there. Only five minutes to turn the cosmos inside out.

Very slowly and carefully he repacked the suitcase and put it in the rack and sat down to think.

What to do?

Accuse Lundgard to his face—no, the man undoubtedly carried that needler. And there was Valeria to think of. A ricocheting dart, a scratch on her, no! It took Bo a long time to decide; his brain seemed viscous. When he looked out of a port to the indifferent stars, he shuddered.

They came back, shedding their spacesuits in the airlock; frost whitened the armor as moisture condensed on chilled surfaces. The metal seemed to breathe cold. Valeria went efficiently to work, stowing the boxed instruments as carefully as if they were her children. There was a laughter on her lips which turned Bo's heart around inside him.

Lundgard leaned over the tiny desk where he sat. "What y' doing?" he asked.

"Recalculating our orbit to Luna," said Bo. "I want to go slow to hyperbolic speed."

Why? It'll add days to the trip, and the fuel—"

"I . . . I'm afraid we might barge into Swarm 770. It's supposed to be near here now and, uh, the positions of those things are never known for sure . . . perturbations . . ." Bo's mouth felt dry.

"You've got a megamile of safety margin or your orbit would never have been approved," argued Lundgard.

"Hell damn it, I'm the captain!" yelled Bo.

"All right, all right . . . take it easy, skipper," Lundgard shot a humorous glance at Valeria. "I certainly don't mind a few extra days in . . . the present company."

She smiled at him. Bo felt ill.

His excuse was thin; if Lundgard thought to check the ephemeris, it would fall to ruin. But he couldn't tell the real reason.

An iron-drive ship does not need to drift along the economical Hohmann "A" orbit of the big freighters; it can build up such furious speed that the sun will swing it along a hyperbola rather than an ellipse, and can still brake that speed near its destination. But the critical stage of acceleration has to be just right, or there will not be enough fuel to stop completely; the ship will be pulled into a cometary orbit and run helpless, the crew probably starving before a rescue vessel can locate them. Bo dared not risk the trouble exploding at full drive; he would drift along, capture and bind Lundgard at the first chance, and then head for Earth. He could handle the *Sirius* alone even if it was illegal; he could not handle her if he had to fight simultaneously.

His knuckles were white on the controls as he loosed the grapples and nudged away from the asteroid with a whisper of power. After a few minutes of low acceleration, he cut the rockets, checked position and velocity, and nodded. "On orbit," he said mechanically. "It's your turn to cook, Ei . . . Einar."

Lundgard swooped easily through the air into the cubbyhole which served for a galley. Cooking in free fall is an art which not all spacemen master, but he could—his meals were even good. Bo felt a helpless kind of rage at his own clumsy efforts.

He crouched in midair, dark of mind, a leg hooked around a stanchion to keep from drifting.

When someone touched him, his heart jumped and he whirled around.

"What's the matter, Bo?" asked Valeria. "You look like doomsday."

"I . . . I . . ." He gulped noisily and twisted his mouth into a smile. Just feeling a little off."

"It's more than that, I think." Her eyes were grave. "You've seemed so unhappy the whole trip. Is there anything I can do to help?"

"Thanks . . . Dr. McKittrick . . . but—"

"Don't be so formal," she said, almost wistfully. "I don't bite. Too many men think I do. Can't we be friends?"

"With a thick-headed clinker like me?" His whisper was raw.

"Don't be silly. It takes brains to be a spaceman. I like a man who knows when to be quiet." She lowered her eyes, the lashes were long and sooty black. "There's something solid about you, something so few people seem to have these days. I wish you wouldn't go feeling so inferior."

At any other time it would have been a sunburst in him. Now he thought of death, and mumbled something and looked away. A hurt expression crossed her face. "I won't bother you," she said gently, and moved off.

The thing was to fall on Lundgard while he slept—

The radar alarm buzzed during a dinner in which Lundgard's flow of talk had battered vainly against silence and finally given up. Bo vaulted over to the control panel and checked. No red light glowed, and the autopilot wasn't whipping them out of danger, so they weren't on a collision course. But the object was getting close. Bo calculated it was an asteroid on an orbit almost parallel to their own, relative speed only a few feet per second; it would come within ten miles or so. In the magnifying periscope, it showed as a jagged dark cube, turning around itself and flashing hard glints of sunlight off mica beds—perhaps six miles square, all crags and cracks and fracture faces, heatless and lifeless and kindless.

Lundgard yawned elaborately after dinner. "Excuse," he said. "Unless somebody's for chess?" His hopeful glance met the grimness of Bo and the odd sadness of Valeria, and he shrugged. "All right, then. Pleasant dreams."

After ten minutes—*now!*

Bo uncoiled himself. "Valeria," he whispered, as if the name were holy.

"Yes?" She ached her brows expectantly.

"I can't stop to explain now. I've got to do something dangerous. Get back aft of the gyro housing."

"What?"

"Get back!" Command blazed frantically in him. "And stay there, whatever happens."

Something like fear flickered in her eyes. It was a very long way to human help. Then she nodded, puzzled but with an obedience which held gallantry, and slipped out of sight behind the steel pillar.

Bo launched himself across the room in a single null-gee bound. One hand ripped aside Lundgard's curtain, the other got him by the throat.

What the hell—"

Lundgard exploded into life. His fist crashed against Bo's cheek. Bo held on with one hand and slugged with the other. Knuckles bounced on rubbery muscle. Lundgard's arm snaked for the tunic stretched on his bunk wall; his body came lithely out of the sack. Bo snatched for that wrist. Lundgard's free hand came around, edged out to slam him in the larynx.

Pain ripped through Bo. He let go and sailed across the room. Lundgard was pulling out his needler.

Bo hit the opposite wall and rebounded—not for the armed man, but for the control panel. Lundgard spat a dart at him. It burst on to the viewport over his shoulder, and Bo caught the acrid whiff of poison. Then the converter was roaring to life and whining gyros spun the ship around.

Lundgard was hurled across the room. He collected himself, catlike, grabbed a stanchion, and raised the gun again. "I've got the drop," he said. "Get away from there or you're a dead man."

It was as if someone else had seized Bo's body. Decision was like lightning through

him. He had tried to capture Lundgard, and
failed, and venom crouched at his back. But
the ship was pointed for the asteroid now,
where it hung gloomily a dozen miles off, and
the rockets were ready to spew.

"If you shoot me," said Bo, "I'll live just
long enough to pour on the juice. We'll hit that
rock and scatter from hell to breakfast."

Valeria emerged. Lundgard swung the
needler to cover her. "Stay where you are!" he
rapped.

"What's happening?" she said fearfully.

"I don't know, said Lundgard, Bo's gone
crazy—attacked me—"

Wrath boiled back in the pilot. He snarled,
"You killed my partner. You must'a been
fixing to kill us too."

"What do you mean?" whispered Valeria.

"How should I know?" said Lundgard.
"He's jumped his orbit, that's all. Look, Bo, be
reasonable. Get away from that panel—"

"Look in his suitcase, Valeria." Bo forced
the words out of a tauntened throat. "A
Venusian shot my partner. You'll find his face
and his clothes in Lundgard's things. I'd know
that face in the middle of the sun."

She hung for a long while, not moving. Bo
couldn't see her. His eyes were nailed to the
asteroid, keeping the ship's nose pointed at it.

"Is that true, Einar?" she asked finally.

"No," said. "Of course not. I do have
Venusian clothes and a mask, but—"

Then why are you keeping me covered too?"

Lundgard didn't answer at once. The only

noise was the murmur of machinery and the dense breathing of three pairs of lungs. Then his laugh jarred forth.

"All right," he said. "I hadn't meant it to come yet, or to come this way, but all right."

"Why did you kill Johnny?" Tears stung Bo's eyes. He never hurt you."

"It was necessary." Lundgard's mouth twitched. "But you see, we knew you were going to Achilles to pick up Valeria and her data. We needed to get a man aboard your ship, to take over when her orbit brought her close to our asteroid base. You've forced my hand—I wasn't going to capture you for days yet. I sabotaged the *Drake's* fuel tanks to get myself stranded there, and shot your friend to get his berth. I'm sorry."

"Why?" Horror rode Valeria's voice.

"I'm a Humanist. I've never made a secret of that. What our secret is, is that some of us aren't content just to talk revolution. We want to give this rotten, over-mechanized society the shove that will bring on its end. We've built up a small force, not much as yet, not enough to accomplish anything lasting. But if we had a solar power beam it would make a big difference. It could be adapted to direct military uses, as well as supplying energy to our machines. A lens effect, a concentration of solar radiation strong enough to burn. Well, it seems worth trying."

"And what do you intend for us?"

"You'll have to be kept prisoners for a while, of course," said Lundgard. "It won't be onerous. We aren't beasts."

"No," said Bo. "Just murderers."

"Save the dramatics," snapped Lundgard.
"I have the gun. Get away from those
controls."

Bo shook his head. There was a wild hammering in his breast, but his voice surprised
him with steadiness: "No. I've got the upper
hand. I can kill you if you move. Yell if he tries
anything, Valeria."

Lundgard's eyes challenged her. "Do you
want to die?" he asked.

Her head lifted. "No," she said, "but I'm not
afraid to. Go ahead if you must, Bo. It's all
right."

Bo felt cold. He knew he wouldn't. He was
bluffing. In the final showdown he could not
crash her. He had seen too many withered
space drained mummies in his time. But
maybe Lundgard didn't realize that.

"Give up," he said. "You can't gain a damn
thing. I'm not going to see a billion people
burned alive just to save our necks. Make a
bargain for your life."

"No," said Lundgard with a curious gentle-
ness. "I have my own brand of honor. I'm not
going to surrender to you. You can't sit there
forever."

Impasse. The ship floated through eternal
silence while they waited.

"All right," said Bo. "I'll fight you for the
power beam."

"How's that?"

"I can throw this ship into orbit around the asteroid. We can go down there and settle the thing between us. The winner can jump up here again with the help of a jet of tanked air. The lump hasn't got much gravity."

Lundgard hesitated. "And how do I know you'll keep your end of the bargain?" he asked. "You could let me go through the airlock, then close it and blast off."

Bo had had some such thought, but he might have known it wouldn't work. "What do you suggest?" he countered, never taking his eyes off the planetoid. "Remember, I don't trust you either."

Lundgard laughed suddenly, a hard yelping bark. "I know! Valeria, go aft and remove all the control-rod links and spares. Bring them back here, I'll go out first, taking half of them with me, and Bo can follow with the other half. He'll have to."

"I—no! I won't," she whispered. "I can't let you—"

"Go ahead and do it," said Bo. He felt a sudden vast weariness. It's the only way we can break this deadlock."

She wept as she went toward the engine room.

Lundgard's thought was good. Without linked control-rods, the converter couldn't operate five minutes, it would flare up and melt itself and kill everyone aboard in a flood of radiation. Whoever won the duel could quickly re-install the necessary parts.

There was a waiting silence. At last Lundgard said, almost abstractedly: "Holmgang. Do you know what that means, Bo?"

"No."

"You ought to. It was a custom of our ancestors back in the early Middle Ages—the Viking time. Two men would go off to a little island, a holm, to settle their differences; one would come back. I never thought it could happen out here." He chuckled bleakly. "Valkyries in spacesuits?"

The girl came back with the links tied in two bundles. Lundgard counted them and nodded. "All right." He seemed strangely calm, an easy assurance lay over him like armor. Bo's fear was cold in his belly, and Valeria wept still with a helpless horror.

The pilot used a safe two minutes of low blast to edge up to the asteriod, "I'll go into the airlock and put on my spacesuit," said Lundgard. "Then I'll jump down and you can put the ship in orbit. Don't try anything while I'm changing, because I'll keep this needler handy."

"It won't work against a spacesuit," said Bo.

Lundgard laughed. "I know," he said. He kissed his hand to Valeria and backed into the lock chamber. The outer valve closed behind him.

"Bo!" Valeria grabbed the pilot by the shoulders, and he looked around into her face. "You can't go out there, I won't let you, I—"

"If I don't," he said tonelessly, "we'll orbit

around here till we starve."

"But you could be killed!"

"I hope not. For your sake, mostly, I hope not," he said awkwardly. "But he won't have any more weapon than me, just a monkey wrench." There was a metal tube welded to the leg of each suit for holding tools; wrenches, the most commonly used, were simply left there as a rule. "I'm bigger than he is."

"But—" She laid her head on his breast and shuddered with crying. He tried to comfort her.

"All right," he said at last. "All right. Lundgard must be through. I'd better get started."

"Leave him!" she blazed. "His air won't last many hours. We can wait."

"And when he sees he's been tricked, you think he won't wreck those links? No. There's no way out."

It was as if all his life he had walked on a road which had no turnings, which led inevitably to this moment.

He made some careful calculations from the instrument readings, physical constants of the asteroid, and used another minute's maneuvering to assume orbital velocity. Alarm lights blinked angry eyes at him, the converter was heating up. No more traveling till the links were restored.

Bo floated from his chair toward the lock. Good-bye, Valeria," he said, feeling the bloodless weakness of words. "I hope it won't be for long."

She threw her arms about him and kissed him. The taste of tears was still on his lips when he had dogged down his helmet.

Opening the outer valve he moved forth, magnetic boots clamping to the hull. A gulf of stars yawned around him, a cloudy halo about his head. The stillness was smothering.

When he was "over" the asteroid he gauged his position with a practiced eye and jumped free. Falling, he thought mostly of Valeria.

As he landed he looked around. No sign of Lundgard. The man could be anywhere in these square miles of cosmic wreckage. He spoke tentatively into his radio, in case Lundgard should be within the horizon: "Hello, are you there?"

"Yes, I'm coming." There was a sharp cruel note of laughter. "Sorry to play this dirty, but there are bigger issues at stake than you or me. I've kept a rifle in my tooltube all the time . . . just in case. Good-bye, Bo."

A slug smashed into the pinnacle behind him. Bo turned and ran.

VI

As he rose over the lip of the crater, his head swung, seeking his enemy. There! It was almost a reflex which brought his arm back and sent the wrench hurtling across the few yards between. Before it had struck, Bo's feet lashed against the pit edge, and the kick arced him toward Lundgard.

Spacemen have to be good at throwing things. The wrench hit the lifted rifle in a

soundless shiver of metal, tore it loose from
an insecure gauntleted grasp and sent it
spinning into shadow. Lundgard yelled, spun
on his heel, and dove after it. Then the flying
body of Bo Jonsson struck him.

Even in low-gee, matter has all its inertia.
The impact rang and boomed within their
armor, they swayed and fell to the ground,
locking arms and hammering futilely at
helmets. Rolling over, Bo got on top, his
hands closed on Lundgard's throat—where
the throat should have been, but plastic and
alloy held fast; instinct had betrayed him.

Lundgard snarled, doubled his legs and
kicked. Bo was sent staggering back. Lundgard crawled erect and turned to look for the
rifle. Bo couldn't see it either in the near-solid
blackness where no light fell, but his wrench
lay as a dark gleam. He sprang for that, closed
a hand on it, bounced up, and rushed at Lundgard. A swing shocked his own muscles with
its force, and Lundgard lurched.

Bo moved in on him. Lundgard reached into
his tool-tube and drew out his own wrench.
He circled, his panting hoarse in Bo's earphones.

"This . . . is the way . . . it was supposed to
be," said Bo.

He jumped in, his weapon whirling down to
shiver again on the other helmet. Lundgard
shook a dazed head and countered. The
impact roared and echoed in Bo's helmet, on
into his skull. He smashed heavily.
Lundgard's lifted wrench parried the blow, it

slid off. Like a fencer, Lundgard snaked his shaft in and the reverberations were deafening.

Bo braced himself and smote with all his power. The hit sang back through iron and alloy, into his own bones. Lundgard staggered a little, hunched himself and struck in return.

They stood with feet braced apart, trading fury, a metal rain on shivering plastic. The stuff was almost unbreakable, but not quite, not for long when such violence dinned on it. Bo felt a lifting wild glee, something savage he had never known before leaped up in him and he bellowed. He was stronger, he could hit harder. Lundgard's helmet would break first!

The Humanist retreated, using his wrench like a sword, stopping the force of blows without trying to deal more of his own. His left hand fumbled at his side. Bo hardly noticed. He was pushing in, hewing, hewing. Again the shrunken sun rose, to flash hard light off his club.

Lundgard grinned, his face barely visible as highlight and shadow behind the plastic. His raised tool turned one hit, it slipped along his arm to rap his flank. Bo twisted his arm around, beat the other wrench aside for a moment, and landed a crack like a thunderbolt.

Then Lundgard had his drinking hose free, pointing in his left hand. He thumbed down the clamp, exposing water at fifty degrees to naked space.

It rushed forth, driven by its own vapor

pressure, a stream like a lance in the wan sun-shine. When it hit Bo's helmet, most of it boiled off . . . cooling the rest, which froze instantly.

Blindness clamped down on Bo. He leaped away, cursing, the front of his helmet so frosted he could not see before him. Lundgard bounced around, playing the hose on him. Through the rime-coat, Bo could make out only a grayness.

He pawed at it, trying to wipe it off, knowing that Lundgard was using this captured minute to look for the rifle. As he got some of the ice loose, he heard a sharp yell of victory—found!

Turning, he ran again.

Over that ridge! Down on your belly! A slug pocked the stone above him. Rolling over, he got to his feet and bounded off toward a steep rise, still wiping blindness off his helmet. But he could not wipe the bitter vomit taste of defeat out of his mouth.

His breathing was a file that raked in his throat. Heart and lungs were ready to tear loose, and there was a cold knot in his guts. Fleeing up the high, ragged slope, he sobbed out his rage at himself and his own stupidity.

At the top of the hill he threw himself to the ground and looked down again over a low wall of basalt. It was hard to see if anything moved down in that valley of night. Then the sun threw a broken gleam off polished metal, the rifle barrel, and he saw Einar Lundgard walking around, looking for him.

The voice came dim in his earphones. "Why don't you give up, Bo? I tell you, I don't want to kill you."

"Yeh." Bo panted wearily. "I'm sure."

"Well, you can never tell," said Lundgard mildly. "It would be rather a nuisance to have to keep not only the fair Valeria, but you, tied up all the way to base. Still, if you'll surrender by the time I've counted ten—"

"Look here," said Bo desperately. "I've got half the links. If you don't give up I'll hammer 'em all flat, and let you starve."

"And Valeria?" The voice jeered at him. He knew his secret was read. "I shouldn't have let you bluff me in the first place. It won't happen a second time. All right: one, two, three—"

Bo could get off this asteroid with no more than the power of his own legs; a few jets from the emergency blow valve at the bottom of an air tank would correct his flight as needed to bring him back to the *Sirius*. He wanted to get up there, and inside warm walls, and take Valeria in his hands and never let her go again. He wanted to live.

"—six, seven, eight—"

He looked at his gauges. A lot of oxyhelium mixture was gone from the tanks, but they were big and there was still several atmospheres' pressure in each. A couple of hours life. If he didn't exert himself too much. They screwed directly into valves in the back of his armor, and—

"—ten. All right, Bo." Lundgard started

moving up the slope, light and graceful as a bird. It was wide and open, no place to hide and sneak up behind him.

Figures reeled through Bo's mind, senselessly. Mass of the asteroid, effective radius, escape velocity only a few feet per second, and he was already on one of the highest points. Brains! he thought with a shattering sorrow. A lot of good mine have done me!

He prepared to back down the other side of the hill, run as well as he could, as long as he could, until a bullet splashed his blood or suffocation thickened it. But I want to fight! he thought through a gulp of tears. I want to stand up and fight!

Orbital velocity equals escape velocity divided by the square root of two.

For a moment he lay there, rigid, and his eyes stared at death walking up the slope but did not see it.

Then, in a crazy blur of motion, he brought his wrench around, closed it on a nut at one side, and turned.

The right hand air tank unscrewed easily. He held it in his hands, a three foot cylinder, blind while calculation raced through his head. What would the centrifugal and Coriolis forces be? It was the roughest sort of estimate. He had neither time nor data, but—

Lundgard was taking it easy, stopping to examine each patch of shadow thrown by some gaunt crag, each meteor scar where a man might hide. It would take him several minutes to reach the hilltop.

Bo clutched the loosened tank in his arms, throwing one leg around it to make sure, and faced away from Lundgard. He hefted himself, as if his body were a machine he must use. Then, carefully, he jumped off the top of the hill.

It was birdlike, dreamlike, thus to soar noiseless over iron desolation. Then sun fell behind him. A spearhead pinnacle clawed after his feet. The Southern Cross flamed in his eyes.

Downward—get rid of that downward component of velocity. He twisted the tank, pointing it toward the surface, and cautiously opened the blow valve with his free hand. Only a moment's exhaust, everything gauged by eye. Did he have an orbit now?

The ground dropped sharply off to infinity, and he saw stars under the keel of the world. He was still going out, away. Maybe he had miscalculated his jump, exceeded escape velocity after all, and was headed for a long cold spin toward Jupiter. It would take all his compressed air to correct such a mistake.

Sweat prickled in his armpits. He locked his teeth and refused to open the valve again.

It was like endless falling, but he couldn't yet be sure if the fall was toward the asteroid or the stars. The rock spun past him. Another face came into view. Yes, by all idiot gods, its gravity was pulling him around!

He skimmed low over the bleakness of it, seeing darkness and starlit death sliding

beneath him. Another crag loomed suddenly
in his path, and he wondered in a harsh clutch
of fear if he was going to crash. Then it
ghosted by, a foot from his flying body. He
thought he could almost sense the chill of it.

He was a moon now, a satellite skimming
low above the airless surface of his own
midget world. The fracture plain where Lundgard had shot at him went by, and he braced
himself. Up around the tiny planet, and there
was the hill he had left, stark against
Sagittarius. He saw Lundgard, standing on its
heights and looking the way he had gone.
Carefully, he aimed the tank and gave himself
another small blast to correct his path. There
was no noise to betray him, the asteroid was a
grave where all sound was long buried and
frozen.

He flattened, holding his body parallel to
the tank in his arms. One hand still gripped
the wrench, the other reached to open the
blow valve wide.

The surge almost tore him loose. He had a
careening lunatic moment of flight in which
the roar of escaping gas boiled through his
armor and he clung like a troll to a runaway
witch's broom. The sun was blinding on one
side of him.

He struck Lundgard with an impact of
velocity and inertia which sent him spinning
down the hill. Bo hit the ground, recoiled, and
sprang after his enemy. Lundgard was still
rolling. As Bo approached, he came to a halt,
lifted his rifle dazedly, and had it knocked

loose with a single blow of the wrench.

Lundgard crawled to his feet while Bo picked up the rifle and threw it off the asteroid. "Why did you do that?"

"I don't know," said Bo. "I should just shoot you down, but I want you to surrender."

Lundgard drew his wrench. "No," he said.

"All right," said Bo. "It won't take long."

When he got up to the *Sirius*, using a tank Lundgard would never need, Valeria had armed herself with a kitchen knife. "It wouldn't have done much good," he said when he came through the airlock. She fell into his arms, sobbing, and he tried to comfort her. "It's all over. All taken care of. We can go home now."

He himself was badly in need of consolation. The inquiry on Earth would clear him, of course, but he would always have to live with the memory of a man stretched dead under a wintery sky. He went aft and replaced the links. When he came back, Valeria had recovered herself, but as she watched his methodical preparations and listened to what he had to tell, there was that in her eyes which he hardly dared believe.

Not him. Not a big dumb slob like him.

One plot was foiled but the struggle continued for another generation. The en-lightened attitudes the Institute sought to implant met increasing cultural and emotional resistance. No amount of psycho-dynamic manipulation could make pure rationality congenial to the average person. Despair deepened as employment rates shrank. The rage of Earth's superfluous masses finally exploded against the gifted elite in the Humanist Revolt of 2170. The Psycho-technic Institute was abolished and its surviving members fled into exile. But like many conquerors before them, the Humanists soon learned it is harder to keep power than to win it.

COLD VICTORY

It was the old argument, Historical Necessity versus the Man of Destiny. When I heard them talking, three together, my heart twisted within me and I knew that once more I must lay down the burden of which I can never be rid.

This was in the Battle Rock House, which is a quiet tavern on the edge of Syrtis Town. I come there whenever I am on Mars. It is friendly and unpretentious: shabby, comfortable loungers scattered about under the massive sandwood rafters, honest liquor and competent chess and the talk of one's peers.

As I entered, a final shaft of thin hard sunlight stabbed in through the window, dazzling me, and then night fell like a thunderclap over the ocherous land and the fluoros snapped on. I got a mug of porter and strolled across to

165

the table about which the three people sat.

The stiff little bald man was obviously from the college; he wore his academics even here, but Martians are like that. "No, no," he was saying. "These movements are too great for any one man to change them appreciably. Humanism, for example, was not the political engine of Carnarvon; rather, he was the puppet of Humanism, and danced as the blind brainless puppeteer made him."

"I'm not so sure," answered the man in gray, undress uniform of the Order of Planetary Engineers. "If he and his cohorts had been doctrinaire, the government of Earth might still be Humanist!"

"But being born of a time of trouble, Humanism was inevitably fanatical," said the professor.

The big, kilted Venusian woman shifted impatiently. She was packing a gun and her helmet was on the floor beside her. Lucifer Clan, I saw from the tartan. "If there are folk around at a crisis time with enough force, they'll shape the way things turn out," she declared. "Otherwise things will drift."

I rolled up a lounger and set my mug on the table. Conversational kibitzing is accepted in the Battle Rock. "Pardon me, gentles," I said. "Maybe I can contribute."

"By all means, Captain," said the Martian, his eyes flickering over my Solar Guard uniform and insignia. "Permit me: I am Professor Freylinghausen—Engineer Buwono; Freelady Neilsen-Singh."

"Captain Crane." I lifted my mug in a formal toast. "Mars, Luna, Venus, and Earth in my case . . . highly representative, are we not? Between us, we should be able to reach a conclusion."

"To a discussion in a vacuum!" snorted the amazon.

"Not quite," said the engineer. "What did you wish to suggest, Captain?"

I got out my pipe and began stuffing it. "There's a case from recent history—the anti-Humanist counterrevolution, in fact—in which I had a part myself. Offhand, at least, it seems a perfect example of sheer accident determining the whole future of the human race. It makes me think we must be more the pawns of chance than of law."

"Well, Captain," said Freylinghausen testily, "let us hear your story and then pass judgment."

"I'll have to fill you in on some background." I lit my pipe and took a comforting drag. I needed comfort just then. It was not to settle an argument that I was telling this, but to reopen an old hurt which would never let itself be forgotten. "This happened during the final attack on the Humanists—"

"A perfect case of inevitability, sir," interrupted Freylinghausen. "May I explain? Thank you. Forgive me if I repeat obvious facts. Their arrangements and interpretation are perhaps not so obvious.

"Psychotechnic government had failed to

solve the problems of Earth's adjustment to living on a high technological level. Conditions worsened until all too many people were ready to try desperate measures. The Humanist revolution was the desperate measure that succeeded in being tried. A typical reaction movement, offering a return to a less intellectualized existence; the savior with the time machine, as Toynbee once phrased it. So naturally its leader, Carnarvon, got to be dictator of the planet.

"But with equal force it was true that Earth could no longer *afford* to cut back her technology. Too many people, too few resources. In the several years of their rule, the Humanists failed to keep their promises; their attempts led only to famine, social disruption, breakdown. Losing popular support, they had to become increasingly arbitrary, thus alienating the people still more.

"At last the oppression of Earth became so brutal that the democratic governments of Mars and Venus brought pressure to bear. But the Humanists had gone too far to back down. Their only possible reaction was to pull Earth-Luna out of the Solar Union.

"We could not see that happen, sir. The lesson of history is too plain. Without a Union council to arbitrate between planets and a Solar Guard to enforce its decisions—there will be war until man is extinct. Earth could not be allowed to secede. Therefore, Mars and Venus aided the counterrevolutionary, anti-Humanist cabal that wanted to restore liberty and Union membership to the mother planet. Therefore, too, a space fleet was raised to support the uprising when it came.

"Don't you see? Every step was an unavoidable consequence, by the logic of survival, of all that had gone before."

"Correct so far, Professor," I nodded. "But the success of the counterrevolution and the Mars-Venus intervention was by no means guaranteed. Mars and Venus were still frontiers, thinly populated, only recently made habitable. They didn't have the military potential of Earth.

"The cabal was well organized. Its well-timed mutinies swept Earth's newly created pro-Humanist ground and air forces before it. The countryside, the oceans, even the cities were soon cleared of Humanist troops.

"But Dictator Carnarvon and the men still loyal to him were holed up in a score of fortresses. Oh, it would have been easy enough to dig them out or blast them out—except that the navy of sovereign Earth, organized from seized units of the Solar Guard, had also remained loyal to Humanism. Its cinc, Admiral K'ung, had acted promptly when the revolt began, jailing all personnel he wasn't sure of ... or shooting them. Only a few got away.

"So there the pro-Union revolutionaries were, in possession of Earth but with a good five hundred enemy warships orbiting above them. K'ung's strategy was simple. He broadcast that unless the rebels surrendered inside one week—or if meanwhile they made any attempt on Carnarvon's remaining strongholds—he'd start bombarding with nuclear weapons. That, of course, would kill perhaps a hundred millon civilians, flatten the factories, poison the sea ranches . . . he'd turn the planet into a butcher shop.

"Under such a threat, the general population was no longer backing the Union cause. They clamored for surrender; they began raising armies. Suddenly the victorious rebels had enemies not merely in front and above them, but behind . . . everywhere!

"Meanwhile, as you all know, the Unionist fleet under Dushanovitch-Alvarez had rendezvoused off Luna; as mixed a bunch of Martians, Venusians, and freedom-minded Earthmen as history ever saw. They were much inferior both in strength and organization; it was impossible for them to charge in and give battle with any hope of winning . . . but Dushanovitch-Alvarez had a plan. It depended on luring the Humanist fleet out to engage him.

"Only Admiral K'ung wasn't having any. The Unionist command knew, from deserters, that most of his captains wanted to go out and annihilate the invaders first, returning to deal with Earth at their leisure. It was a costly nuisance, the Unionists sneaking in, firing and retreating, blowing up ship after ship of the Humanist forces. But K'ung had the final word, and he would not accept the challenge until the rebels on the ground had capitulated. He was negotiating with them now, and it looked very much as if they would give in.

"So there it was, the entire outcome of the war—the whole history of man, for if you will pardon my saying so, gentles, Earth is still the key planet—everything hanging on this one officer, Grand Admiral K'ung Li-Po, a grim man who had given his oath and had a damnably good grasp of the military facts of life."

I took a long draught from my mug and began the story, using the third-person form which is customary on Mars.

The speedster blasted at four gees till she was a bare five hundred kilometers from the closest enemy vessels. Her radar screens jittered with their nearness and in the thunder of abused hearts her crew sat waiting for the doomsday of a homing missle. Then she was at the calculated point, she spat her cargo out the main lock and leaped ahead still more furiously. In moments the thin glare of her jets was lost among crowding stars.

The cargo was three spacesuited men, linked to a giant air tank and burdened with a variety of tools. The orbit into which they had been flung was aligned with that of the Humanist fleet, so that relative velocity was low.

In cosmic terms, that is. It still amounted to nearly a thousand kilometers per hour and was enough, unchecked, to spatter the men against an armored hull.

Lieutenant Robert Crane pulled himself along the light cable that bound him, up to the tank. His hands groped in the pitchy gloom of shadowside. Then all at once rotation had brought him into the moonlight and he could see. He found the rungs and went hand over hand along the curve of the barrel, centrifugal force streaming his body outward. Damn the clumsiness of space armor! Awkwardly, he got one foot into a stirrup-like arrangement and scrambled around until he was in the "saddle" with both boots firmly locked; then he unclipped the line from his waist.

The stars turned about him in a cold majestic wheel. Luna was nearly at the full, ashen pale, scored and pocked and filling his helmet with icy luminescence. Earth was an enormous grayness in the sky, a half ring of blinding light from the hidden sun along one side.

Twisting a head made giddy by the spinning, he saw the other two mounted behind him. García was in the middle—you could always tell a Venusian; he painted his clan markings on his suit—and the Martian Wolf at the end. "Okay," he said, incongruously aware that the throat mike pinched his Adam's apple, "let's stop this merry-go-round."

His hands moved across a simple control panel. A tangentially mounted nozzle opened, emitting an invisible stream of air. The stars slowed their lunatic dance, steadied . . . hell and sunfire, now he'd overcompensated, give it a blast from the other side . . . the tank was no longer in rotation. He was not hanging head downward, but falling, a long weightless tumble through a sterile infinity.

Three men rode a barrel of compressed air toward the massed fleet of Earth.

"Any radar reading?" García's voice was tinny in the earphones.

"A moment, if you please, till I have it set up." Wolf extended a telescoping mast, switched on the portable 'scope, and began sweeping the sky. "Nearest indication . . . um . . . one o'clock, five degrees low, four hundred twenty-two kilometers distant." He added radial and linear velocity, and García worked an astrogator's slide rule, swearing at the tricky light.

The base line was not the tank, but its velocity, which could be assumed straight-line for so short a distance. Actually, the weird horse had its nose pointed a full thirty degrees off the direction of movement. "High" and "low," in weightlessness, were simply determined by the plane bisecting the tank, with the men's heads arbitrarily designated as "aimed up."

The airbarrel had jets aligned in three planes, as well as the rotation-controlling tangential nozzles. With Wolf and García to correct him, Crane blended vectors until they were on a course that would nearly intercept the ship. Gas was released from the forward jet at a rate calculated to match velocity.

Crane had nothing but the gauges to tell him that he was braking. Carefully dehydrated air emerges quite invisibly, and its ionization is negligible; there was no converter to radiate, and all equipment was painted a dead nonreflecting black.

Soundless and invisible—too small and fast for a chance eye to see in the uncertain moonlight, for a chance radar beam to register as anything worth buzzing an alarm about. Not enough infrared for detection, not enough mass, no trail of ions—the machinists on the *Thor* had wrought well, the astrogators had figured as closely as men and computers are able. But in the end it was only a tank of compressed air, a bomb, a few tools, and three men frightened and lonely.

"How long will it take us to get there?" asked Crane. His throat was dry and he swallowed hard.

"About forty-five minutes to that ship we're zeroed in on," García told him. "After that, *quien sabe?* We'll have to locate the *Monitor.*"

"Be most economical with the air, if you please," said Wolf. "We also have to get back."

"Tell me more," snorted Crane.

"If this works," remarked García, "we'll have added a new weapon to the System's arsenals. That's why I volunteered. If Antonio García of Hesperus gets his name in the history books, my whole clan will contribute to give me the biggest ranch on Venus."

They were an anachronism, thought Crane, a resurrection from old days when war was a wilder business. The psychotechs had not picked a team for compatibility, nor welded them into an unbreakable brotherhood. They had merely grabbed the first three willing to try an untested scheme. There wasn't time for anything else. In another forty hours, the pro-Union armies on Earth would either have surrendered or the bombardment would begin.

"Why are you lads here?" went on the Venusian. "We might as well get acquainted."

"I took an oath," said Wolf. There was nothing priggish about it; Martians thought that way.

"What of you, Crane?"

"I . . . it looked like fun," said the Earthman lamely. "And it might end this damned war."

He lied and he knew so, but how do you explain? Do you admit it was an escape from your shipmates' eyes?

Not that his going over to the rebels had shamed him. Everyone aboard the *Marduk* had done so, except for a couple of CPO's who were now under guard in Aphrodite. The cruiser had been on patrol off Venus when word of Earth's secession had flashed. Her captain had declared for the Union and the Guard to which he belonged, and the crew cheered him for it.

For two years, while Dushanovitch-Alvarez, half idealist and half buccaneer, was assembling the Unionist fleet, intelligence reports trickled in from Earth. Mutiny was being organized, and men escaped from those Guard vessels—the bulk of the old space

service—that had been at the mother planet
and were seized to make a navy. Just before
the Unionists accelerated for rendezvous, a
list of the new captains appointed by K'ung
had been received. And the skipper of the
Huitzilopochli was named Benjamin Crane.

Ben . . . what did you do when your brother
was on the enemy side? Dushanovitch-Alvarez
had let the System know that a bombardment
of Earth would be regarded as genocide and
all officers partaking in it would be punished
under Union law. It seemed unlikely that
there would be any Union to try the case, but
Lieutenant Robert Crane of the *Marduk* had
protested: this was not a normal police
operation, it was war, and executing men who
merely obeyed the government they had
pledged to uphold was opening the gates to a
darker barbarism than the fighting itself. The
Unionist forces was too shorthanded, it could
not give Lieutenant Crane more than a public
reproof for insubordination, but his mess-
mates had tended to grow silent when he
entered the wardroom.

If the superdreadnaught *Monitor* could be
destroyed, and K'ung with it, Earth might not
be bombarded. Then if the Unionists won, Ben
would go free, or he would die cleanly in
battle—reason enough to ride this thing into
the Humanist fleet!

Silence was cold in their helmets.

"I've been thinking," said García. "Suppose
we do carry this off, but they decide to blast
Earth anyway before dealing with our boats.

What then?"

"Then they blast Earth," said Wolf. "Though most likely they won't have to. Last I heard, the threat alone was making folk rise against our friends on the ground there." Moonlight shimmered along his arm as he pointed at the darkened planet-shield before them. "So the Humanists will be back in power, and even if we chop up their navy, we won't win unless we do some bombarding of our own."

"*Madre de Dios!*" García crossed himself, a barely visible gesture in the unreal flood of undiffused light. "I'll mutiny before I give my name to such a thing."

"And I," said Wolf shortly. "And most of us, I think."

It was not that the Union fleet was crewed by saints, thought Crane. Most of its personnel had signed on for booty; the System knew how much treasure was locked in the vaults of Earth's dictators. But the horror of nuclear war had been too deeply graven for anyone but a fanatic at the point of desperation to think of using it.

Even in K'ung's command, there must be talk of revolt. Since his ultimatum, deserters in lifeboats had brought Dushanovitch-Alvarez a mountain of precise information. But the Humanists had had ten years in which to build a hard cadre of hard young officers to keep the men obedient.

Strange to know that Ben was with them—*why?*

I haven't seen you in more than two years now, Ben—nor my own wife and children, but tonight it is you who dwell in me, and I have not felt such pain for many years. Not since that time we were boys together, and you were sick one day, and I went alone down the steep bluffs above the Mississippi. There I found the old man denned up under the trees, a tramp, one of many millions for whom there was no place in this new world of shining machines— but he was not embittered, he drew his citizen's allowance and tramped the planet and he had stories to tell me which our world of bright hard metal had forgotten. He told me about Br'er Rabbit and the briar patch; never had I heard such a story, it was the first time I knew the rich dark humor of the earth itself. And you got well, Ben, and I took you down to his camp, but he was gone and you never heard the story of Br'er Rabbit. On that day, Ben, I was as close to weeping as I am right this night of murder.

The minutes dragged past. Only numbers went between the three men on the tank, astrogational corrections. They sat, each in his own skull with his own thoughts.

The vessel on which they had zeroed came into plain view, a long black shark swimming against the Milky Way. They passed within two kilometers of her. Wolf was busy now, flicking his radar around the sky, telling off ships. It was mostly seat-of-the-pants piloting, low relative velocities and small distances, edging into the mass of Earth's fleet. That was

not a very dense mass; kilometers gaped
between each unit. The *Monitor* was in the
inner ring; a deserter had given them the
approximate orbit.

"You're pretty good at this, boy," said
García.

"I rode a scooter in the asteroids for a
couple of years," answered Crane. "Patrol
and rescue duty."

That was when there had still been only the
Guard, one fleet and one flag. Crane had never
liked the revolutionary government of Earth,
but while the Union remained and the only
navy was the Guard and its only task to help
any and all men, he had been reasonably
content. Please God, that day would come
again.

Slowly, over the minutes, the *Monitor* grew
before him, a giant spheroid never meant to
land on a planet. He could see gun turrets
scrawled black across remote star-clouds.
There was more reason for destroying her
than basic strategy—luring the Humanists
out to do batle; more than good tactics—built
only last year, she was the most formidable
engine of war in the Solar System. It would be
the annihilation of a symbol. The *Monitor*,
alone among ships that rode the sky, was
designed with no other purpose than killing.

Slow, now, easy, gauge the speeds by eye,
remember how much inertia you've got . . .
Edge up, brake, throw out a magnetic anchor
and grapple fast. Crane turned a small winch,
the cable tautened and he bumped against

the hull.

Nobody spoke. They had work to do, and their short-range radio might have been detected. García unshipped the bomb. Crane held it while the Venusian scrambled from the saddle and got a firm boot-grip on the dreadnaught. The bomb didn't have a large mass. Crane handed it over, and García slapped it onto the hull, gripped by a magnetic plate. Stooping, he wound a spring and jerked a lever. Then, with a spaceman's finicking care, he returned to the saddle. Crane paid out the cable till it ran off the drum; they were free of their grapple.

In twenty minutes, the clockwork was to set off the bomb. It was a little one, plutonium fission, and most of its energy would be wasted on vacuum. Enough would remain to smash the *Monitor* into a hundred fragments.

Crane worked the airjets, forcing himself to be calm and deliberate. The barrel swung about to point at Luna, and he opened the rear throttle wide. Acceleration tugged at him, he braced his feet in the stirrups and hung on with both hands. Behind them, the *Monitor* receded, borne on her own orbit around a planet where terror walked.

When they were a good fifteen kilometers away, he asked for a course. His voice felt remote, as if it came from outside his prickling skin. Most of him wondered just how many men were aboard the dreadnaught and how many wives and children they had to weep for them. Wolf squinted through a

sextant and gave his readings to García.
Corrections made, they rode toward the point
of rendezvous: a point so tricky to compute, in
this Solar System where the planets were
never still, that they would doubtless not
come within a hundred kilometers of the
speedster that was to pick them up. But they
had a hand-cranked radio that would broadcast a signal for the boat to get a fix on them.

How many minutes had they been going?
Ten . . . ? Crane looked at the clock in the
control panel. Yes, ten. Another five or so, at
this acceleration, ought to see them beyond
the outermost orbit of the Humanist ships—

He did not hear the explosion. A swift and
terrible glare opened inside his helmet,
enough light reflected off the inner surface
for his eyes to swim in white-hot blindness.
He clung to his seat, nerves and muscles
tensed against the hammer blow that never
came. The haze parted raggedly, and he
turned his head back toward Earth. A wan
nimbus of incadescent gas hung there. A few
tattered stars glowed blue as they fled from it.

Wolf's voice whispered in his ears: "She's
gone already. The bomb went off ahead of
schedule. Something in the clockwork—"

"But she's gone!" García let out a rattling
whoop. "No more flagship. We got her, lads,
we got the stinking can!"

Not far away was a shadow visible only
when it blocked off the stars. A ship . . . light
cruiser— "Cram on the air!" said Wolf
roughly. "Let's get the devil out of here."

"I can't." Crane snarled it, still dazed, wanting only to rest and forget every war that ever was. "We've only got so much pressure left, and none to spare for maneuvering if we get off course."

"All right ..." They lapsed into silence. That which had been the *Monitor*, gas and shrapnel, dissipated. The enemy cruiser fell behind them, and Luna filled their eyes with barren radiance.

They were not aware of pursuit until the squad was almost on them. There were a dozen men in combat armor, driven by individual jet-units and carrying rifles. They overhauled the tank and edged in—less gracefully than fish, for they had no friction to kill forward velocity, but they moved in.

After the first leap of his heart, Crane felt cold and numb. None of his party bore arms: they themselves had been the weapon, and now it was discharged. In a mechanical fashion, he turned his headset to the standard band.

"Rebels ahoy!" The voice was strained close to breaking, an American voice. . . . For a moment such a wave of homesickness for the green dales of Wisconsin went over Crane that he he could not move nor realize he had been captured. "Stop that thing and come with us!"

In sheer reflex, Crane opened the rear throttles full. The barrel jumped ahead, almost ripping him from the saddle. Ions flared behind as the enemy followed. Their

the radio, Mr. Nicholson, and report what has happened. In the meantime, I'll question the prisoner myself. Privately."

"Yes, sir." The officer saluted and went out. There was compassion in his eyes.

Ben closed the door behind him. Then he turned around and floated, crossing his legs, one hand on a stanchion and the other rubbing his forehead. His brother had known he would do exactly that. *But how accurately can he read me?*

"Well, Bob." Ben's tone was gentle.

Robert Crane shifted, feeling the link about his ankle. "How are Mary and the kids?" he asked.

"Oh . . . quite well, thank you. I'm afraid I can't tell you much about your own family. Last I heard, they were living in Manitowoc Unit, but in the confusion since . . ." Ben looked away. "They were never bothered by our police, though. I have some little influence."

"Thanks," said Robert. Bitterness broke forth: "Yours are safe in Luna City. Mine will get the fallout when you bombard, or they'll starve in the famine to follow."

The captain's mouth wrenched. "Don't say that!" After a moment: "Do you think I like the idea of shooting at Earth? If you so-called liberators really give a curse in hell about the people their hearts bleed for so loudly, they'll surrender first. We're offering terms. They'll be allowed to go to Mars or Venus."

"I'm afraid you misjudge us, Ben," said

Robert. "Do you know why I'm here? It wasn't simply a matter of being on the *Marduk* when she elected to stay with the Union. I believed in the liberation."

"Believe in those pirates out there?" Ben's finger stabbed at the wall, as if to pierce it and show the stars and the hostile ships swimming between.

"Oh, sure, they've been promised the treasure vaults. We had to raise men and ships somehow. What good was that money doing, locked away by Carnarvon and his gang?" Robert shrugged. "Look, I was born and raised in America. We were always a free people. The Bill of Rights was molded on our own old Ten Amendments. From the moment the Humanists seized power, I had to start watching what I said, who I associated with, what tapes I got from the library. My kids were growing up into perfect little parrots. It was too much. When the purges began, when the police fired on crowds rioting because they were starving—and they were starving because this quasi-religious creed cannot accept the realities and organize things rationally—I was only waiting for my chance.

"Ben, be honest. Wouldn't you have signed on with us if you'd been on the *Marduk?*"

The face before him was gray. "Don't ask me that! No!"

"I can tell you exactly why not, Ben." Robert folded his arms and would not let his brother's eyes go. "I know you well enough. We're different in one respect. To you, no principle can be as important as your wife and children—and they're hostages for your good behavior. Oh, yes, K'ung's psychotechs evaluated you very carefully. Probably half their captains are held by just such chains."

Ben laughed, a loud bleak noise above the murmur of the ventilators. "Have it your way. And don't forget that your family is alive, too, because I stayed with the government. I'm not going to change, either. A government, even the most arbitrary one, can perhaps be altered in time. But the dead never come back to life."

He leaned forward, suddenly shuddering. "Bob, I don't want you sent Earthside for interrogation. They'll not only drug you, they'll set about changing your whole viewpoint. Surgery, shock, a rebuilt personality— you won't be the same man when they've finished.

"I can wangle something else. I have enough pull, especially now in the confusion after your raid, to keep you here. When the war is settled, I'll arrange for your escape. There's going to be so much hullaballoo on Earth that nobody will notice. But you'll have to help me, in turn.

"*What was the real purpose of your raid? What plans does your high command have?*"

For a time which seemed to become very long, Robert Crane waited. He was being asked to betray his side voluntarily; the alternative was to do it anyway, after the psychmen got through with him. Ben had no authority to make the decision. It would mean court-martial later, and punishment visited on his family as well, unless he could justify it by claiming quicker results than the long-drawn process of narcosynthesis.

The captain's hands twisted together, big knobby hands, and he stared at them. "This is a hell of a choice for you, I know," he mumbled. "But there's Mary and . . . the kids, and men here who trust me. Good decent men. We aren't fiends, believe me. But I can't deny my own shipmates a fighting chance to get home alive."

Robert Crane wet his lips. "How do you know I'll tell the truth?" he asked.

Ben looked up again, crinkling his eyes. "We had a formula once," he said. "Remember? 'Cross my heart and hope to die, spit in my eye if I tell a lie.' I don't think either of us ever lied when we took that oath."

"And— Ben, the whole war hangs on this, maybe. Do you seriously think I'd keep my word for a kid's chant if it could decide the war?"

"Oh, no." A smile ghosted across the captain's mouth. "But there's going to be a meeting of skippers, if I know Hokusai. He'll want the opinions of us all as to what we should do next. Having heard them, he'll make his own decision. I'll be one voice among a lot of others.

"But if I can speak with whatever information you've given me . . . do you understand? The council will meet long before you could be sent Earthside and quizzed. I need your knowledge *now*. I'll listen to whatever you have to say. I may or may not believe you . . . I'll make my own decision as to what to recommend . . . but it's the only way I can save you, and myself, and everything else I care about.''

He waited then, patiently as the circling ships. They must have come around the planet by now, thought Robert Crane. The sun would be drowning many stars, and Earth would be daylit if you looked out.

Captains' council. . . . It sounded awkward and slow, when at any moment, as far as they knew, Dushanovitch-Alvarez might come in at the head of his fleet. But after all, the navy would remain on general alert, second officers would be left in charge. They had time.

And they would want time. Nearly every one of them had kin on Earth. None wished to explode radioactive death across the world they loved. K'ung's will had been like steel, but now they would—subconsciously, and the more powerfully for that—be looking for any way out of the frightful necessity. A respected officer, giving good logical reasons for postponing the bombardment, would be listened to by the keenest ears.

Robert Crane shivered. It was a heartless load to put on a man. The dice of future history . . . he could load the dice, because he knew Ben as any man knows a dear brother, but maybe his hand would slip while he loaded them.

"Well?" It was a grating in the captain's throat.

Robert drew a long breath. "All right," he said.

"Yes?" A high, cracked note; Ben must be near breaking, too.

"I'm not in command, you realize." Robert's words were blurred with haste. "I can't tell for sure what— But I do know we've got fewer ships. A lot fwer."

"I suspected that."

"We have some plan—I haven't been told what—it depends on making you leave this orbit and come out and fight us where we are. If you stay home, we can't do a damn thing. This raid of mine . . . we'd hope that your admiral dead, you'd join battle out toward Luna."

Robert Crane hung in the air, twisting in its currents, the breath gasping in and out of him. Ben looked dim, across the room, as if his eyes were failing.

"Is that the truth, Bob?" The question seemed to come from light-years away.

"Yes. Yes. I can't let you go and get killed and— Cross my heart and hope to die, spit in my eye if I tell a lie!"

I set down my mug, empty, and signaled for another. The bartender glided across the floor with it and I drank thirstily, remembering how my throat had felt mummified long ago on the *Huitzilopochtli*, remembering much else.

"Very well, sir." Freylinghausen's testy voice broke a stillness. "What happened?"

"You ought to know that, Professor," I replied. "It's in the history tapes. The Humanist fleet decided to go out at once and dispose of its inferior opponent. Their idea—correct, I suppose—was that a space victory would be so demoralizing that the rebels on the ground would captiulate immediately after. It would have destroyed the last hope of reinforcements, you see."

"And the Union fleet won," said Neilsen-Singh. "They chopped the Humanist navy into fishbait. I know. My father was there. We bought a dozen new reclamation units with his share of the loot, afterward."

"Naval history is out of my line, Captain Crane," said the engineer, Buwono. "How did Dushanovitch-Alvarez win?"

"Oh . . . by a combination of things. Chiefly, he disposed his ships and gave them such velocities that the enemy, following the usual principles of tactics, moved at high accelerations to close in. And at a point where they would have built up a good big speed, he had a lot of stuff planted, rocks and ball bearings and scrap iron . . . an artificial meteoroid swarm, moving in an opposed orbit. After that had done its work, the two forces were on very nearly equal strength, and it became a battle of standard weapons. Which Dushanovitch-Alvarez knew how to use! A more brilliant naval mind hasn't existed since Lord Nelson."

"Yes, yes," said Freylinghausen impatiently. "But what has this to do with the subject under discussion?"

"Don't you see, Professor? It was chance right down the line—chance which was skillfully exploited when it arose, to be sure, but nevertheless a set of unpredictable accidents. The *Monitor* blew up ten minutes ahead of schedule; as a result, the commando that did it was captured. Normally, this would have meant that the whole plan would have been given away. I can't emphasize too strongly that the Humanists would have won if they'd only stayed where they were."

I tossed off a long gulp of porter, knocked the dottle from my pipe, and began refilling it. My hands weren't quite steady. "But chance entered here, too, making Robert Crane's brother the man to capture him. And Robert knew how to manipulate Ben. At the captain's council, the *Huitzilopochtli's* skipper spoke the most strongly in favor of going out to do battle. His arguments, especially when everyone knew they were based on information obtained from a prisoner, convinced the others."

"But you said . . ." Neilsen-Singh looked confused.

"Yes, I did." I smiled at her, though my thoughts were entirely in the past. "But it wasn't till years later that Ben heard the story of Br'er Rabbit and the briar patch; he came across it in his brother's boyhood diary. Robert Crane told the truth, swore to it by a boyhood oath—but his brother could not

believe he'd yield so easily. Robert was almost
begging him to stay with K'ung's original
plan. Ben was sure that was an outright
lie . . . that Dushanovitch-Alvarez must
actually be planning to attack the navy in its
orbit and could not possibly survive a battle
in open space. So that, of course, was what he
argued for at the council."

"It took nerve, though," said Neilsen-Singh.
"Knowing what the *Huitzilopochtli* would
have to face . . . knowing you'd be aboard,
too. . . .'"

"She was a wreck by the time the battle was
over," I said. "Not many in her survived."

After a moment, Buwono nodded thoughtfully. "I see your point, Captain. The accident
of the bomb's going off too soon almost
wrecked the Union plan. The accident of that
brotherhood saved it. A thread of coinci-
dences . . . yes, I think you've proved your
case."

"I'm afraid not, gentles." Freylinghausen
darted birdlike eyes around the table. "You
misunderstood me. I was not speaking of
minor ripples in the mainstream of history.
Certainly those are ruled by chance. But the
broad current moves quite inexorably, I
assure you. *Vide:* Earth and Luna are back in
the Union under a more or less democratic
government, but no solution has yet been
found to the problems which brought forth
the Humanists. They will come again; under
one name or another they will return. The war
was merely a ripple."

"Maybe." I spoke with inurbane curtness, not liking the thought. "We'll see."

"If nothing else," said Neilsen-Singh, "you people bought for Earth a few more decades of freedom. They can't take that away from you."

I looked at her with sudden respect. It was true. Men died and civilizations died, but before they died they lived. No effort was altogether futile.

I could not remain here, though. I had told the story, as I must always tell it, and now I needed aloneness.

"Excuse me." I finished my drink and stood up. "I have an appointment . . . just dropped in . . . very happy to have met you, gentles."

Buwono rose with the others and bowed formally. "I trust we shall have the pleasure of your company again, Captain Robert Crane."

"Robert—? Oh." I stopped. I had told what I must in third person, but everything had seemed so obvious. "I'm sorry. Robert Crane was killed in the battle. I am Captain Benjamin Crane, at your service, gentles."

I bowed to them and went out the door. The night was lonesome in the streets and across the desert.

Captain Crane's melancholy was shared by many in that unhappy era. The Humanist solution had failed but so had the Institute's. Rebel disclosures of the faltering Institute's sordid and illegal machinations had turned public opinion against it permanently. Although reviving the organization was unthinkable, strictly regulated "tame" psychotechnicians continued to serve the victorious Union government. The majority of Earthlings grudgingly accepted their dependence on advanced technology but felt no more satisfied with their lot than before the Revolt. Some consoled themselves with private pleasures; other searched quietly for new solutions. The surviving research institutions fell under closer scrutiny lest they succumb to the same corruption as the Psychotechnic Institute. Science was to be held accountable both for what it could do and for what it should do.

WHAT SHALL IT PROFIT?

"The chickens got out of the coop and flew away three hundred years ago," said Barwell. "Now they're coming home to roost."

He hiccoughed. His finger wobbled to the dial and clicked off another whisky. The machine pondered the matter and flashed an apologetic sign: *Please deposit your money*.

"Oh, damn," said Barwell. "I'm broke."

Radek shrugged and gave the slot a two-credit piece. It slid the whisky out on a tray with his change. He stuck the coins in his pouch and took another careful sip of beer.

Barwell grabbed the whisky glass like a drowning man. He *would* drown, thought Radek, if he sloshed much more into his stomach.

There was an Asian whine to the music

drifting past the curtains into the booth. Radek could hear the talk and laughter well enough to catch their raucous overtones. Somebody swore as dice rattled wrong for him. Somebody else shouted coarse good wishes as his friend took a hostess upstairs.

He wondered why vice was always so cheerless when you went into a place and paid for it.

"I am going to get drunk tonight," announced Barwell. "I am going to get so high in the stony sky you'll need radar to find me. Then I shall raise the red flag of revolution."

"And tomorrow?" asked Radek quietly.

Barwell grimaced. "Don't ask me about tomorrow. Tomorrow I will be among the great leisure class—to hell with euphemisms —the unemployed. Nothing I can do that some goddam machine can't do quicker and better. So a benevolent state will feed me and clothe me and house me and give me a little spending money to have fun on. This is known as citizen's credit. They used to call it a dole. Tomorrow I shall have to be more systematic about the revolution—join the League or something."

"The trouble with you," Radek needled him, "is that you can't adapt. Technology has made the labor of most people, except the first-rank creative genius, unnecessary. This leaves the majority with a void of years to fill somehow—a sense of uprootedness and lost self-respect—which is rather horrible. And in any case, they don't like to think in scientific terms . . . it doesn't come natural to the average man."

Barwell gave him a bleary stare out of a flushed, sagging face. "I s'pose you're one of the geniuses," he said. "You got work."

"I'm adaptable," said Radek. He was a slim youngish man with dark hair and sharp features. "I'm not greatly gifted, but I found a niche for myself. Newsman. I do legwork for a major commentator. Between times, I'm writing a book—my own analysis of contemporary historical trends. It won't be anything startling, but it may help a few people think more clearly and adjust themselves."

"And so you *like* this rotten Solar Union?" Barwell's tone became aggressive.

"Not everything about it no. So there is a wave of antiscientific reaction, all over Earth. Science is being made the scapegoat for all our troubles. But like it or not, you fellows will have to accept the fact that there are too many people and two few resources for us to survive without technology."

"Some technology, sure," admitted Barwell. He took a ferocious swig from his glass. "Not this hell-born stuff we've been monkeying around with. I tell you, the chickens have finally come home to roost."

Radek was intrigued by the archaic expression. Barwell was no moron: he'd been a correlative clerk at the Institute for several years, not a position for fools. He had read, actually read books, and thought about them.

And today he had been fired. Radek chanced

across him drinking out a vast resentment and attached himself like a reverse lamprey—buying most of the liquor. There might be a story in it, somewhere. There might be a lead to what the Institute was doing.

Radek was not antiscientific, but neither did he make gods out of people with technical degrees. The Institute *must* be up to something unpleasant . . . otherwise, why all the mystery? If the facts weren't uncovered in time, if whatever they were brewing came to a head, it could touch off the final convulsion of lynch law.

Barwell leaned forward, his finger wagged. "Three hundred years now. I think it's three hundred years since X-rays came in. Damn scientists, fooling around with X-rays, atomic energy, radioactives . . . sure, safe levels, established tolerances, but what about the long-range effects? What about cumulative genetic effects? Those chickens are coming home at last."

"No use blaming our ancestors," said Radek. "Be rather pointless to go dance on their graves, wouldn't it?"

Barwell moved closer to Radek. His breath was powerful with whisky. "But are they in those graves?" he whispered.

"Huh?"

"Look. Been known for a long time, ever since first atomic energy work . . . heavy but nonlethal doses of radiation shorten lifespan. You grow old faster if you get a strong dose. Why d'you think with all our medicines we're not two, three hundred years old? Back-ground count's gone up, that's why! Radioactives in the air, in the sea, buried under the ground. Gamma rays, not *entirely* absorbed by shielding. Sure, sure, they tell us the level is still harmless. But it's more than the level in nature by a good big factor—two or three."

Radek sipped his beer. He'd been drinking slowly, and the beer had gotten warmer than he liked, but he needed a clear head. "That's common knowledge," he stated. "The lifespan hasn't been shortened any, either."

"Because of more medicines . . . more ways to help cells patch up radiation damage. All but worst radiation sickness been curable for a long time." Barwell waved his hand expansively. "They knew, even back then," he mumbled. "If radiation shortens life, radiation sickness cures ought to prolong it. Huh? Reas'nable? Only the goddam scientists . . . population problem . . . social stasis if ever'body lived for centuries . . . kept it secret. Easy t' do. Change y'r name and face ever' ten, twen'y years—keep to y'rself, don't make friends among the short-lived, you might see 'em grow old and die, might start feelin' sorry for 'em an' that would never do, would it—?"

Coldness tingled along Radek's spine. He lifted his mug and pretended to drink. Over the rim, his eyes stayed on Barwell.

"Tha's why they fired me. I know. I know. I got ears. I overheard things. I read . . . notes

not inten'ed for me. They fired me. 'S a
wonder they didn' murder me." Barwell
shuddered and peered at the curtains, as if
trying to look through them. "Or d'y'
think—maybe—"

"No," said Radek. "I don't. Let's stick to the
facts. I take it you found mention of work
on— shall we say—increasing the lifespan.
Perhaps a mention of successes with rats and
guinea pigs. Right? So what's wrong with
that? They wouldn't want to announce anything till they were sure, or the hysteria—"

Barwell smiled with an irritating air of
omniscience. "More'n that, friend. More'n
that. Lots more."

"Well, what?"

Barwell peered about him with exaggerated
caution. One thing I found in files . . . plans of
whole buildin's an' groun's—great, great big
room, lotsa rooms, way way underground.
Secret. Only th' kitchen was makin' food an'
sendin' it down there—human food. Food for
people I never saw, people who never came
up—" Barwell buried his face in his hands.
"Don' feel so good. Whirlin'—"

Radek eased his head to the table. Out like a
spent credit. The newsman left the booth and
addressed a bouncer. "Chap in there has had
it."

"Uh-huh. Want me to help you get him to
your boat?"

"No. I hardly know him." A bill exchanged
hands. "Put him in your dossroom to sleep it
off, and give him breakfast with my compli-

ments. I'm going out for some fresh air."

The rec house stood on a Minnesota bluff, overlooking the Mississippi River. Beyond its racket and multi-colored glare, there was darkness and wooded silence. Here and there the lights of a few isolated houses gleamed. The river slid by, talking, ruffled with moonlight. Luna was nearly full; squinting into her cold ashen face, Radek could just see the tiny spark of a city. Stars were strewn carelessly over heaven, he recognized the ember that was Mars.

Perhaps he ought to emigrate. Mars, Venus, even Luna . . . there was more hope on them than Earth had. No mechanical packaged cheer: people had work to do, and in their spare time made their own pleasures. No civilization cracking at the seams because it could not assimilate the technology it must have; out in space, men knew very well that science had carried them to their homes and made those homes fit to dwell on.

Radek strolled across the parking lot and found his airboat. He paused by its iridescent teardrop to start a cigaret.

Suppose the Institute of Human Biology was more than it claimed to be, more than a set of homes and laboratories where congenial minds could live and do research. It published discoveries of value—but how much did it not publish? Its personnel kept pretty aloof from the rest of the world, not unnatural in this day of growing estrangement between science and public . . . but did they have a deeper reason than that?

Suppose they did keep immortals in those underground rooms.

A scientist was not ordinarily a good political technician. He might react emotionally against a public beginning to throw stones at his house and consider taking the reins . . . for the people's own good, of course. A lot of misery had been caused the human race for its own alleged good.

Or if the scientist knew how to live forever, he might not think Joe Smith or Carlos Ibañez or Wang Yuan or Johannes Umfanduma good enough to share immorality with him.

Radek took a long breath. The night air felt fresh and alive in his lungs after the tavern staleness.

He was not currently married, but there was a girl with whom he was thinking seriously of making a permanent contract. He had friends, not lucent razor minds but decent, unassuming, kindly people, brave with man's old quiet bravery in the face of death and ruin and the petty tragedies of everyday. He liked beer and steaks, fishing and tennis, good music and a good book and the exhilarating strain of his work. He liked to live.

Maybe a system for becoming immortal, or at least living many centuries, was not desirable for the race. But only the whole race had authority to make that decision.

Radek smiled at himself, twistedly, and threw the cigaret away and got into the boat.

Its engine murmured, sucking 'cast power; the riding lights snapped on automatically and he lifted into the sky. It was not much of a lead he had, but it was as good as he was ever likely to get.

He set the autopilot for southwest Colorado and opened the jets wide. The night whistled darkly around his cabin. Against wan stars, he made out the lamps of other boats, flitting across the world and somehow intensifying the loneliness.

Work to do. He called the main office in Dallas Unit and taped a statement of what he knew and what he planned. Then he dialed the nearest library and asked the robot for information on the Institute of Human Biology.

There wasn't a great deal of value to him. It had been in existence for about 250 years, more or less concurrently with the Psycho-technic Institute and for quite a while affiliated with that organization. During the Humanist troubles, when the Psychotechs were booted out of government on Earth and their files ransacked, it had dissociated itself from them and carried on unobtrusively. (How much of their secret records had it taken along?) Since the Restoration, it had grown, drawing in many prominent research-ers and making discoveries of high value to medicine and bio-engineering. The current director was Dr. Marcus Lang, formerly of New Harvard, the University of Luna, and— No matter. He'd been running the show for eight years, after his predecessor's death.

Or had Tokogama really died?

He couldn't be identical with Lang—he had been a short Japanese and Lang was a tall Negro, too big a jump for any surgeon. Not to mention their simultaneous careers. But how far back could you trace Lang before he became fakeable records of birth and schooling? What young fellow named Yamatsu or Hideki was now polishing glass in the labs and slated to become the next director?

How fantastic could you get on how little evidence?

Radek let the text fade from the screen and sat puffing another cigaret. It was a while before he demanded references on the biology of the aging process.

That was tough sledding. He couldn't follow the mathematics or the chemistry very far. No good popularizations were available. But a newsman got an ability to winnow what he learned. Radek didn't have to take notes, he'd been through a mind-training course; after an hour or so, he sat back and reviewed what he had gotten.

The living organism was a small island of low entropy in a universe tending constantly toward gigantic disorder. It maintained itself through an intricate set of hemostatic mechanisms. The serious disruption of any of these brought the life-processes to a halt. Shock, disease, the bullet in the lungs or the ax in the brain—death.

But hundreds of thousands of autopsies had

never given an honest verdict of "death from old age." It was always something else, cancer, heart failure, sickness, stroke . . . age was at most a contributing cause, decreasing resistance to injury and power to recover from it.

One by one, the individual causes had been licked. Bacteria and protozoa and viruses were slaughtered in the body. Cancers were selectively poisoned. Cholesterol was dissolved out of the arteries. Surgery patched up damaged organs, and the new regeneration techniques replaced what had been lost . . . even nervous tissue. Offhand, there was no more reason to die, unless you met murder or an accident.

But people still grew old. The process wasn't as hideous as it had been. You needn't shuffle in arthritic feebleness. Your mind was clear, your skin wrinkled slowly. Centenarians were not uncommon these days. But very few reached 150. Nobody reached 200. Imperceptibly, the fires burned low . . . vitality was diminished, strength faded, hair whitened, eyes dimmed. The body responded less and less well to regenerative treatment. Finally it did not respond at all. You got so weak that some small thing you and your doctor could have laughed at in your youth, took you away.

You still grew old. And because you grew old, you still died.

The unicellular organism did not age. But "age" was a meaningless word in that particular case. A man could be immortal via his germ cells. The micro-organism could too, but it gave the only cell it had. Personal immorality was denied to both man and microbe.

Could sheer mechanical wear and tear be the reason for the decline known as old age? Probably not. The natural regenerative powers of life were better than that. And observations made in free fall, where strain was minimized, indicated that while null-gravity had an alleviating effect, it was no key to living forever.

Something in the chemistry and physics of the cells themselves, then. They did tend to accumulate heavy water—that had been known for a long time. Hard to see how that could kill you . . . the percentage increase in a lifetime was so small. It might be a partial answer. You might grow old more slowly if you drank only water made of pure isotopes. But you wouldn't be immortal.

Radek shrugged. He was getting near the end of his trip. Let the Institute people answer his questions.

The Four Corners country is so named because four of the old American states met there, back when they were still significant political units. For a while, in the 20th century, it was overrun with uranium hunters, who made small impression on its tilted emptiness. It was still a favorite vacation area, and the resorts were lost in that great huddle of mountains and desert. You could have a lot of privacy here.

Gliding down over the moon-ghostly Pueblo ruins of Mesa Verde, Radek peered through the windscreen. There, ahead. Lights glowed around the walls, spread across half a mesa. Inside them was a parkscape of trees, lawns, gardens, arbors, cottage units . . . the Institute housed its people well. There were four large buildings at the center, and Radek noted gratefully that several windows were still shining in them. Not that he had any compunctions about getting the great Dr. Lang out of bed, but—

He ignored the public landing field outside the walls and set his boat down in the paved courtyard.

As he climbed out, half a dozen guards came running. They were husky men in blue uniforms, armed with stunners, and the dim light showed faces hinting they wouldn't be sorry to feed him a beam. Radek dropped to the ground, folded his arms, and waited. The breath from his nose was frosty under the moon.

"What the hell do you want?"

The nearest guard pulled up in front of him and laid a hand on his shock gun. "Who the devil are you? Don't you know this is private property? What's the big idea, anyway?"

"Take it easy," advised Radek. "I have to see Dr. Lang at once. Emergency."

"You didn't call for an appointment, did you?"

"No, I didn't."

"All right, then—"

"I didn't think he'd care to have me give my reasons over a radio. This is confidential and urgent."

The men hesitated, uncertain before such an outrageous violation of all civilized canons. "I dunno, friend . . . he's busy . . . if you want to see Dr. McCormick—"

"Dr. Lang. Ask him if I may. Tell him I have news about his longevity process."

"His what?"

Radek spelled it out and watched the man go. Another one made some ungracious remark and frisked him with needles ostentation. A third was more urbane: "Sorry to do this, but you understand we've got important work going on. Can't have just anybody busting in."

"Sure, that's all right." Radek shivered in the thin chill air and pulled his cloak tighter about him.

"Viruses and stuff around. If any of that got loose— You understand."

Well, it wasn't a bad cover-up. None of these fellows looked very bright. IQ treatments could do only so much, thereafter you got down to the limitations of basic and unalterable brain microstructure. And even among the more intellectual workers . . . how many Barwells were there, handling semi-routine tasks but not permitted to know what really went on under their feet? Radek had a brief irrational wish that he'd worn boots instead of sandals.

The first guard returned. "He'll see you," he grunted. "And you better make it good, because he's one mad doctor."

Radek nodded and followed two of the men. The nearest of the large square buildings seemed given over to offices. He was led inside, down a short length of glow-lit corridor, and halted while the scanner on a door marked, LANG, DIRECTOR observed him.

"He's clean, boss," said one of the escort.

"All right," said the annunciator. "Let him in. But you two stay just outside."

It was a spacious office, but austerely furnished. A telewindow reflected green larches and a sun-spattered waterfall, somewhere on the other side of the planet. Lang sat alone behind the desk, his hands engaged with some papers that looked like technical reports. He was a big, heavy-shouldered man, his hair gray, his chocolate face middle-aged and tired.

He did not rise. "Well?" he snapped.

"My name is Arnold Radek. I'm a news service operator . . . here's my card, if you wish to see it."

"Pharaoh had it easy," said Lang in a chill voice. "Moses only called the seven plagues down on him. I have to deal with your sort."

Radek placed his fingertips on the desk and leaned forward. He found it unexpectedly hard not to be stared down by the other. "I know very well I've laid myself open to a lawsuit by coming in as I did," he stated.

"Possibly, when I'm through, I'll be open to murder."

"Are you feeling well?" There was more contempt than concern in the deep tone.

"Let me say first off, I believe I have information about a certain project of yours. One you badly want to keep a secret. I've taped a record at my office of what I know and where I'm going. If I don't get back before 1000 hours, Central Time, and wipe that tape, it'll be heard by the secretary."

Lang took an exasperated breath. His fingernails whitened on the sheets he still held. "Do you honestly think we would be so . . . I won't say unscrupulous . . . so *stupid* as to use violence?"

"No," said Radek. "Of course not. All I want is a few straight answers. I know you're quite able to lead me up the garden path, feed me some line of pap and hustle me out again—but I won't stand for that. I mentioned my tape only to convince you that I'm in earnest."

"You're not drunk," murmured Lang. "But there are a lot of people running loose who ought to be in a mental hospital."

"I know." Radek sat down without waiting for an invitation. "Anti-scientific fanatics. I'm not one of them. You know Darrell Burkhardt's news commentaries? I supply a lot of his data and interpretations. He's one of the leading friends of genuine science, one of the few you have left." Radek gestured at the card on the desk. "Read it, right there."

Lang picked the card up and glanced at the

lettering and tossed it back. "Very well. That's still no excuse for breaking in like this. You—"

"It can't wait," interrupted Radek. "There are a lot of lives at stake. Every minute we sit here, there are perhaps a million people dying, perhaps more; I haven't the figures. And everyone else is dying all the time, millimeter by millimeter, we're all born dying. Every minute you hold back the cure for old age, you murder a million human beings."

"This is the most fantastic—"

"Let me finish! I get around. And I'm trained to look a little bit more closely at the facts everybody knows, the ordinary commonplace facts we take for granted and never think to inquire about because they are so ordinary. I've wondered about the Institute for a long time. Tonight I talked at great length with a fellow named Barwell . . . remember him? A clerk here. You fired him this morning for being too nosy. He had a lot to say."

"Hm." Lang sat quiet for a while. He didn't rattle easily—he couldn't be snowed under by fast, aggressive talk. While Radek spat out what clues he had, Lang calmly reached into a drawer and got out an old-fashioned briar pipe, stuffed it and lit it.

"So what do you want?" he asked when Radek paused for breath.

"The truth, damn it!"

"There are privacy laws. It was established

long ago that a citizen is entitled to privacy if he does nothing against the common weal—"

"And you are! You're like a man who stands on a river bank and has a lifebelt and won't throw it to a man drowning in the river."

Lang sighed. "I won't deny we're working on longevity," he answered. "Obviously we are. The problem interests biologists throughout the Solar System. But we aren't publicizing our findings as yet for a very good reason. You know how people jump to conclusions. Can you imagine the hysteria that would arise in this already unstable culture if there seemed to be even a prospect of immortality? You yourself are a prime case . . . on the most tenuous basis of rumor and hypothesis, you've decided that we have found a vaccine against old age and are hoarding it. You come bursting in here in the middle of the night, demanding to be made immortal immediately if not sooner. And you're comparatively civilized . . . there are enough lunatics who'd come here with guns and start shooting up the place."

Radek smiled bleakly. "Of course. I know that. And you ought to know the outfit I work for is reputable. If you have a good lead on the problem, but haven't solved it yet, you can trust us not to make that fact public.

"All right." Lang mustered an answering smile, oddly warm and charming. "I don't mind telling you, then, that we do have some promising preliminary results—but, and this is the catch, we estimate it will take at least a century to get anywhere. Biochemistry is an inconceivably complex subject."

"What sort of results are they?"

"It's highly technical. Has to do with enzymes. You may know that enzymes are the major device through which the genes govern the organism all through life. At a certain point, for intance, the genes order the body to go through the changes involved in puberty. At another point, they order that gradual breakdown we know as aging."

"In other words," said Radek slowly, "the body has a built-in suicide mechanism?"

"Well . . . if you want to put it that way—"

"I don't believe a word of it. It makes a lot more sense to imagine that there's something which causes the breakdown—a virus, maybe —and the body fights it off as long as possible but at last it gets the upper hand. The whole key to evolution is the need to survive. I can't see life evolving its own anti-survival factor."

"But nature doesn't care about the individual, friend Radek. Only about the species. And the species with a rapid turnover of individuals can evolve faster, become more effective—"

"Then why does man, the fastest-evolving metazoan of all, have one of the longest life-spans? He does, you know . . . among mammals, at any rate. Seems to me our bodies must be all-around better than average, better able to fight off the death virus. Fish live a longer time, sure—and maybe in the water they aren't so exposed to the disease. May flies are short-lived; have they simply adapted their life cycle to the existence of the virus?"

Lang frowned. "You appear to have studied this subject enough to have some mistaken ideas about it. I can't argue with a man who insists on protecting his cherished irrationalities with fancy verbalisms."

"And you appear to think fast on your feet, Dr. Lang." Radek laughed. "Maybe not fast enough. But I'm not being paranoid about this. You can convince me."

"How?"

"Show me. Take me into those underground rooms and show me what you actually have."

"I'm afraid that's impos—"

"All right." Radek stood up. "I hate to do this, but a man must either earn a living or go on the public freeloading roll . . . which I don't want to do. The facts and conjectures I already have will make an interesting story."

Lang rose too, his eyes widening. "You can't prove anything!"

"Of course I can't. You're sitting on all the proof."

"But the public reaction! God in Heaven, man, those people can't *think!*"

"No . . . they can't, can they?" He moved toward the door. "Goodnight."

Radek's muscles were taut. In spite of everything that had been said, a person hounded to desperation could still do murder.

There was a great quietness as he heard the door. Then Lang spoke. The voice was defeated, and when Radek looked back it was an old man who stood behind the desk.

"You win. Come along with me."

They went down an empty hall, after dismissing the guards, and took an elevator below ground. Neither of them said anything. Somehow, the sag of Lang's shoulders was a gnawing in Radek's conscience.

When they emerged, it was to transfer past a sentry, where Lang gave a password and okayed his companion, to another elevator which purred them still deeper.

"I—" The newsman cleared his throat, awkwardly. "I repeat what I implied earlier. I'm here mostly as a citizen interested in the public welfare . . . which includes my own, of course, and my family's if I ever have one. If you can show me valid reasons for not breaking this story, I won't. I'll even let you hypnocondition me against doing it, voluntarily or otherwise."

"Thanks," said the director. His mouth curved upward, but it was a shaken smile. "That's decent of you, and we'll accept . . . I think you'll agree with our policy. What worries me is the rest of the world. If you could find out as much as you did—"

Radek's heart jumped between his ribs. "Then you do have immortality!"

"Yes. But I'm not immortal. None of our personnel are, except—Here we are."

There was a hidden susurrus of machinery as they stepped out into a small bare entry-room. Another guard sat there, beside a desk. Past him was a small door of immense solidity, the door of a vault.

"You'll have to leave everything metallic here," said Lang. "A steel object could jump so fiercely as to injure you. Your watch would be ruined. Even coins could get uncomfortably hot . . . eddy currents, you know. We're about to go through the strongest magnetic field ever generated."

Silently, dry-mouthed, Radek piled his things on the desk. Lang operated a combination lock on the door. "There are nervous effects too," he said. "The field is actually strong enough to influence the electric discharge of your synapses. Be prepared for a few nasty seconds. Follow me and walk fast."

The door opened on a low, narrow corridor several meters long. Radek felt his heart bump crazily, his vision blurred, there was panic screaming in his brain and sweating tingle in his skin. Stumbling through nightmare, he made it to the end.

The horror faded. They were in another room, with storage facilities and what resembled a spaceship's airlock in the opposite wall. Lang grinned shakily. "No fun, is it?"

"What's it for?" gasped Radek.

"To keep charged particles out of here. And the whole set of chambers is 500 meters underground, sheathed in ten meters of lead brick and surrounded by tanks of heavy water. This is the only place in the Solar System, I imagine, where cosmic rays never come."

"You mean—"

Lang knocked out his pipe and left it in a gobboon. He opened the lockers to reveal a set of airsuits, complete with helmets and oxygen tanks. "We put these on before going any further," he said.

"Infection on the other side?"

"We're the infected ones. Come on, I'll help you."

As they scrambled into the equipment, Lang added conversationally: "This place has to have all its own stuff, of course . . . its own electric generators and so on. The ultimate power source is isotopically pure carbon burned in oxygen. We use a nuclear reactor to create the magnetic field itself, but no atomic energy is allowed inside it." He led the way into the airlock, closed it, and started the pumps. "We have to flush out all the normal air and substitute that from the inner chambers."

"How about food? Barwell said food was prepared in the kitchens and brought here."

"Synthesized out of elements recovered from waste products. We do cook it topside, taking precautions. A few radioactive atoms get in, but not enough to matter as long as we're careful. We're so cramped for space down here we have to make some compromises."

"I think—" Radek fell silent. As the lock was evacuated, his unjointed airsuit spread-eagled and held him prisoner, but he hardly noticed. There was too much else to think about, too much to grasp at once.

Not till the cycle was over and they had
gone through the lock did he speak again.
Then it came harsh and jerky: "I begin to
understand. How long has this gone on?"

"It started about 200 years ago . . . an early
Institute project." Lang's voice was somehow
tinny over the helmet phone. "At that time, it
wasn't possible to make really pure isotopes
in quantity, so there were only limited results,
but it was enough to justify further research.
This particular set of chambers and chemical
elements is 150 years old. A spectacular
success, a brilliant confirmation, from the
very beginning . . . and the Institute has never
dared reveal it. Maybe they should have, back
then—maybe people could have taken the
news—but not now. These days the knowledge would whip men into a murderous rage
of frustration; they wouldn't believe the truth,
they wouldn't dare believe, and God alone
knows what they'd do."

Looking around, Radek saw a large, plastic-
lined room, filled with cages. As the lights
went on, white rats and guinea pigs stirred
sleepily. One of the rats came up to nibble at
the wires and regard the humans from beady
pink eyes.

Lang bent over and studied the label. "This
fellow is, um, 66 years old. Still fat and sassy,
in perfect condition, as you can see. Our
oldest mammalian inmate is a guinea pig: a
hundred and forty-five years. This one here."

Lang stared at the immortal beast for a
while. It didn't look unusual . . . only healthy.

"How about monkeys?" he asked.

"We tried them. Finally gave it up. A monkey is an active animal—it was too cruel to keep them penned up forever. They even went insane, some of them."

Footfalls were hollow as Lang led the way toward the inner door. "Do you get the idea?"

"Yes . . . I think I do. If heavy radiation speeds up aging—then natural radioactivity is responsible for normal aging."

"Quite. A matter of cells being slowly deranged, through decades in the case of man—the genes which govern them being mutilated, chromosomes ripped up, nucleoplasm irreversibly damaged. And, of course, a mutated cell often puts out the wrong combination of enzymes, and if it regenerates at all it replaces itself by one of the same kind. The effect is cumulative, more and more defective cells every hour. A steady bombardment, all your life . . . here on Earth, seven cosmic rays per second ripping through you, and you yourself are radioactive, you include radiocarbon and radiopotassium and radiophosphorus . . . Earth and the planets, the atmosphere, everything radiates. Is it any wonder that at last our organic mechanism starts breaking down? The marvel is that we live as long as we do."

The dry voice was somehow steadying. Radek asked: "And this place is insulated?"

"Yes. The original plant and animal life in here was grown exogenetically from single-cell zygotes, supplied with air and nourishment built from pure stable isotopes. The Institute had to start with low forms, naturally; at that time, it wasn't possible to synthesize proteins to order. But soon our workers had enough of an ecology to intro-duce higher species, eventually mammals. Even the first generation was only negligibly radioactive. Succeeding generations have been kept almost absolutely clean. The lamps supply ultraviolet, the air is recycled . . . well, in principle it's no different from an ecological-unit spaceship."

Radek shook his head. He could scarcely get the words out: "People? Humans?"

"For the past 120 years. Wasn't hard to get germ plasm and grow it. The first generation reproduced normally, the second could if lack of space didn't force us to load their food with chemical contraceptive." Behind his faceplate, Lang grimaced. "I'd never have allowed it if I'd been director at the time, but now I'm stuck with the situation. The legality is very doubtful. How badly do you violate a man's civil rights when you keep him a prisoner but give him immortality?"

He opened the door, an archaic manual type. "We can't do better for them than this," he said. "The volume of space we can enclose in a magnetic field of the necessary strength is already at an absolute maximum."

Light sprang automatically from the ceiling. Radek looked in at a dormitory. It was well-kept, the furniture ornamental. Beyond it he could see other rooms . . . recreation, he supposed vaguely.

The score of hulks in the beds hardly moved. Only one woke up. He blinked, yawned, and shuffled toward the visitors, quite nude, his long hair tangled across the low forehead, a loose grin on the mouth.

"Hello, Bill," said Lang.

"Uh . . . got sumpin? Got sumpin for Bill?" A hand reached out, begging. Radek thought of a trained ape he had once seen.

"This is Bill." Lang spoke softly, as if afraid his voice would snap. "Our oldest inhabitant. One hundred and nineteen years old, and he has the physique of a man of 20. They mature, you know, reach their peak and never fall below it again."

"Got sumpin, doc, huh?"

"I'm sorry, Bill," said Lang. "I'll bring you some candy next time."

The moron gave an animal sigh and shambled back. On the way, he passed a sleeping woman, and edged toward her with a grunt. Lang closed the door.

There was another stillness.

"Well," said Lang, "now you've seen it."

"You mean . . . you don't mean immortality makes you like that?"

"Oh, no. Not at all. But my predecessors chose low-grade stock on purpose. Remember those monkeys. How long do you think a normal human could remain sane, cooped up in a little cave like this and never daring to leave it? That's the only way to be immortal, you know. And how much of the race could be given such elaborate care, even if they could stand it? Only a small percentage. Nor would they live forever—they're already contaminated, they were born radioactive. And whatever happens, who's going to remain outside and keep the apparatus in order?"

Radek nodded. His neck felt stiff, and within the airsuit he stank with sweat. "I've got the idea."

"And yet—if the facts were known—if my questions had to be answered—how long do you think a society like ours would survive?"

Radek tried to speak, but his tongue was too dry.

Lang smiled grimly. "Apparently I've convinced you. Good. Fine." Suddenly his gloved hand shot out and gripped Radek's shoulder. Even through the heavy fabric, the newsman could feel the bruising fury of that clasp.

"But you're only one man," whispered Lang. "An unusually reasonable man for these days. There'll be others.

"What are we going to *do*?"

Meanwhile, far uglier experiments were underway on Ganymede where a few hundred psychotechnicians had fled during the Revolt. The refugees subverted the colony of reactionary cultists already living there and warped their totalitarian society even further. Apparently, the psychotechnicians planned to breed a mindlessly loyal army of genetically modified troops who would restore the Institute to its old position. The conspirators were unmasked early in the twenty-third century by the Planetary Engineers they had hired to terraform Ganymede and Callisto. The Order subsequently took the colonists under its protection until they were ready to function normally.

Half a century later, the Engineers still patiently toiled on Jupiter's moons. But the minions of chaos were as diligent and unyielding in pursuit of their goals as the forces of order. A collision was inevitable.

BRAKE

In that hour, when he came off watch, Captain Peter Banning did not go directly to his cabin. He felt a wish for uninhibited humor, such as this bleak age could not bring to life (except maybe in the clan gatherings of Venus—but Venus was *too* raw), and remembered that Luke Devon had a Shakespeare. It was a long time since Banning had last read *The Taming of the Shrew*. He would drop in and borrow the volume, possibly have a small drink and a chinfest. The Planetary Engineer was unusually worth talking to.

So it was that he stepped out of the companionway into A-deck corridor and saw Devon backed up against the wall at gun point.

Banning had not stayed alive as long as this—a good deal longer than he admit-

ted—through unnecessary heroics. He slid
back, flattened himself against the aluminum
side of the stairwell, and stretched his ears.
Very gently, one hand removed the stubby
pipe from his teeth and slipped it into a
pocket of his tunic, to smolder itself out. The
fumes might give him away to a sensitive
nose, and he was unarmed.

Devon spoke softly, with rage chained in his
throat: "The devil damn thee black, thou
cream-faced loon!"

"Not so hasty," advised the other person. It
was the Minerals Authority representatives,
Serge Andreyev, a large hairy man who
dressed and talked too loudly. "I do not wish
to kill you. This is just a needler in my hand.
But I have also a gun for blowing out brains—
if required."

His English bore its usual accent, but the
tone had changed utterly. It was not the
timbre of an irritating extrovert; there was no
particular melodrama intended; Andreyev
was making a cool statement of fact.

"It is unfortunate for me that you recognized me through all the surgical changes," he
went on. "It is still more unfortunate for you
that I was armed. Now we shall bargain."

"Perhaps." Devon had grown calmer. Banning could visualize him, backed up against
the wall, hands in the air: a tall man, cat-lithe
under the austere stiffness of his Order, close-
cropped yellow hair and ice-blue eyes, and a
prow of nose jutting from the bony face. *I
wouldn't much like to have that hombre on*

my tail, reflected Banning.

"Perhaps," repeated Devon. "Has it occurred to you, though, that a steward, a deckhand . . . anyone . . . may be along at any moment?"

"Just so. Into my cabin. There we shall talk some more."

"But it *is* infernally awkward for you," said Devon. " 'Is it a world to hide virtues in?'—or prisoners, for that matter? Here we are, beyond Mars, with another two weeks before we reach Jupiter. There are a good fifteen people aboard, passengers and crew—not much, perhaps, for a ship as big as the 'Thunderbolt,' but enough to search her pretty thoroughly if anyone disappears. You can't just cram me out any convenient air lock, you know, not without getting the keys from an officer. Neither can you keep me locked away without inquiries as to why I don't show up for meals . . . I assure you, if you haven't noticed, my appetite is notorious. Therefore, dear old chap—"

"We will settle this later," snapped Andreyev. "Quickly, now, go to my cabin. I shall be behind. If necessary, I will needle you and drag you there."

Devon was playing for time, thought Banning. If the tableau of gunman and captive remained much longer in the passageway, someone was bound to come by and— *As a matter of fact, son, someone already has.*

The captain slipped a hand into his pouch. He had a number of coins: not that they'd be any use on Ganymede, but he didn't want to reenter Union territory without beer cash. He selected several of nearly uniform size and tucked them as a stack into his fist. It was a very old stunt.

Then, with the quick precision of a hunter—which he had been now and then, among other things—he glided from the companionway. Andreyev had just turned his back, marching Devon up the hall toward Cabin 5. Peter Banning's weighted fist smote him at the base of the skull.

Devon whirled, a tiger in gray. Banning eased Andreyev to the floor with one hand; the other took the stun pistol, not especially aimed at the Engineer nor especially aimed away from him. "Take it easy, friend," he murmured.

"You . . . oh!" Devon eased, muscle by muscle. A slow grin crossed his face. " 'For this relief, much thanks.' "

"What's going on here?" asked the captain.

There was a moment of stillness. Only the ship spoke, with a whisper of ventilators. The sound might almost have belonged to that night of cold stars through which she hurled.

"Well?" said Banning impatiently.

Devon stood for an instant longer, as if taking his measure. The captain was a stocky man of medium height, with faintly grizzled black hair clipped short on a long head. His face was broad, it bore high cheekbones, and its dark-white skin had a somehow ageless look: deep trenches from wide nose to big

mouth, crow's-feet around the bony-ridged
gray eyes, otherwise smooth as a child's. He
did not wear the trim blue jacket and white
trousers of the Fireball Line but favored a
Venusian-style beret and kilt, Arabian carpet
slippers, a disreputable old green tunic of
possibly Martian origin.

"I don't know," said the Planetary Engineer
at last. "He just pulled that gun on me."

"Sorry, I heard a bit of the talk between
you. Now come clean. I'm responsible for this
ship, and I want to know what's going on."

"So do I," said Devon grimly. "I'm not
really trying to stall you, skipper—not much,
anyway." He stooped over Andreyev and
searched the huddled body. "Ah, yes, here's
that other gun he spoke of, the lethal one."

"Give me that!" Banning snatched it. The
metal was cold and heavy in his grasp. It came
to him with a faint shock that he himself and
his entire crew had nothing more dangerous
between them than some knives and monkey
wrenches. A spaceship was not a Spanish
caravel, her crew had no reason to arm
against pirates or mutiny or—

Or did they?

"Go find a steward," snapped Banning.
"Come back here with him. Mr. Andreyev
goes in irons for the rest of the trip."

"Irons?" Under the cowl of his gray tunic,
Devon's brows went up.

"Chains . . . restraint . . . hell, we'll lock him
away. I've got a bad habit of using archaisms.
Now, jump!"

The Engineer went quickly down the hall. Banning lounged back, twirling the gun by its trigger guard, and watched him go.

Where had he seen the fellow before?

He searched a cluttered memory for a tall blond man who was athlete, technician, Shakespearean enthusiast, and amateur painter in oils. Perhaps it was only someone he had read about, with a portrait; there was so much history—Wait. The Rostomily brotherhood. Of course. But that was three centuries ago!

Presumably someone, somewhere, had kept a few cells in storage, after that corps of exogenetic twins had finally made their secret open, disbanded, and mingled their superior genes in the common human lifestream. And then, perhaps thirty years ago, the Engineers had quietly grown such a child in a tank. Maybe a lot of them. Also anything could happen in that secret castle on the rim of Archimedes Crater, and the Solar System none the wiser till the project exploded in man's collective face.

The brotherhood had been a trump card of the early Un-men, in the days when world government was frail and embattled. A revived brotherhood must be of comparable importance to the Order. But for what purpose? The Engineers, quasi-military, almost religious, were supposed to be above politics; they were supposed to serve all men, an independent force whose only war was against the inanimate cosmos.

Banning felt a chill. With the civilization-splitting tension that existed on Earth and was daily wrung one notch higher, he could imagine what hidden struggles took place between the many factions. It wasn't all psychodynamics, telecampaigning or parliamentary maneuver: the Humanist episode had scarred Earth's soul, and now there were sometimes knives in the night.

Somehow an aspect of those battles had focused on his ship.

He took out his pipe, rekindled it, and puffed hard. Andreyev stirred, with a retch and a rattle in his throat.

There was a light football in the corridor. Banning looked up. He would have cursed the interruption had anyone but Cleonie Rogers appeared. As it was, he made the forgotten gesture of raising his cap.

"Oh!" Her hand went to her mouth. For an instant she looked frightened, then came forward in a way he liked: the more so as she had been consistently annoyed by Andreyev's loud attempts to flirt. "Oh, is he hurt? Can I help?"

"Better stand back, m'lady," advised Banning. She saw the stunner in his hand and the automatic in his waistband. Her lips parted in the large-eyed, snub-nosed face. With the yellow hair that fell softly down to bare shoulders, with a wholly feminine topless shimmergown and a whisper of cosmetics, she was a small walking anachronism.

"What happened?" A shaken courage rallied in her. It was well done, thought the

man, considering that she was a child of
wealth, never done a day's work in her life,
bound for the Jovian Republic as an actual
live tourist.

"That's what I'd kind of like to know," he
told her. "This character here pulled an
equalizer—a gun, I mean—on Engineer
Devon. Then I came along and sapped him."

He saw her stiffen. Even aboard the
"Thunderbolt," which was not one of the
inner-planet luxury liners but a freighter
whose few passengers—except her—were
bound for Ganymede on business . . . even
here there were dimly lit corners and piped
music and the majesty of the stars. Banning
had noticed how much she and Devon had
been together. Therefore he said kindly: "Oh,
Luke wasn't hurt. I sent him for help. Must
say it's taking him one hell of a time, too. Did
the stewards crawl into the fire chamber for a
nap?"

She smiled uncertainly. "What do you think
the trouble is, Captain? Did Mr. Andreyev,
ah—"

"Slip a cog?" Banning scowled. In his pre-
occupation he forgot that the rising incidence
of nonsanity on Earth made the subject unfit
for general conversation. "I doubt it. He came
aboard with these toys, remember. I wonder,
though. Now that the topic has come up, we
do have a rum lot of passengers."

Devon was legitimate enough, his mind continued: a genuine Engineer, nursemaiding the
terraforming equipment which was the

"Thunderbolt's" prime cargo, the great machines which the Order would use to make Europa habitable.

And Cleoniè must be an authentic tourist. (Since he regarded her as a woman, which he did not the crop-headed, tight-lipped, sad-clad creature that was today's typical Western Terrestrial female, Banning thought of her by her first name.) On the other hand—

Andreyev was not a simple Union bureaucrat, sent to negotiate a trade agreement; or, if he was, he was also much more. and how about the big fellow, Robert Falken, allegedly a nucleonic technie offered a job on Callisto? He didn't say much at table, kept to himself, but Banning knew a hard, tough man when he saw one. And Morgan Gentry, astronaut, who said the Republic had hired him to pilot inter-satellite shuttles—undoubtedly a trained spaceman, but what was he besides that? And the exchange professor of advanced symbolics, dome-healed little Gomez, was he really bound for a position at the new University of X?

The girl's voice interrupted his reverie: "Captain Banning . . . what *could* be the matter with the passengers? They're all Westerners, aren't they?"

He could still be shocked, just a little bit every now and then. He hesitated a second before realizing that she had spoken not in ill will but from blank naïveté. "What has that got to do with it?" he said. "You don't really think, do you, Miss, that the conflict on Earth is a simple question of Oriental Kali worshipers versus a puritanical protechnological Occident?" He paused for breath, then plowed on: "Why, the Kali people are only one branch of the Ramakrishian Eclectics, and there are plenty of Asians who stand by population control and Technic civilization—I have a couple in my own crew—and there are Americans who worship the Destroyer as fervently as any Ganges River farmer—and the Husseinite Moslems are closer to you, Miss Rogers, than you are to the New Christendom—"

He broke off, shaking his head. It was too big to be neatly summarized, the schism which threatened to rip Earth apart. He might have said it boiled down to the fact that technology had failed to solve problems which *must* be solved; but he didn't want to phrase it thus, because it would sound antiscientific, and he wasn't.

Thank all kindly gods that there were men on other planets now! The harvest of all the patient centuries since Galileo would not be entirely lost, whatever happened to Earth.

Andreyev pulled himself up till he rested on his hands, head dangling between his shoulders. He groaned.

"I wonder how much of that is put on," mused Banning. "I did a well-caliberated job of slugging him. He shouldn't be too badly concussed." He gave Cleonie a beady look. "Maybe we ought to haul him into a cabin at that. Don't want to rattle any other cash customers, do we? Where are they all, anyway?"

"I'm not sure. I just left my cabin—" She stopped.

Someone came running from aft. The curvature of the hall, which was wrapped around the inner skin of the ship, made it impossible to see more than about forty meters. Banning shifted his gun, warily.

It was the large square-faced man, Falken, who burst into view. "Captain!" he shouted. The metal that enclosed all of them gave his tone a faint, unhuman resonance. "Captain, what happened?"

"How do you *know* about it, son?"

"A . . . eh . . . Engineer Devon—" Falken jogged to a halt, a meter away. "He told me—"

"Told you? Well, did he now?" Banning's gray gaze narrowed. Suddenly the needler in his hand leaped up and found an aim. "Hold it. Hold it there, pardner," and reach."

Falken flushed red. "What the ruination do you mean?"

"I mean that if you even look like you're going after a gun, I'll put you to sleep," said Banning. "Then if it turns out you only intended to offer me a peanut butter sandwich, I'll beg your humble pardon. But something sure smells here."

Falken backed away. "All right, all right, I'll go," he snarled. "I just wanted to help."

Cleonie screamed.

As Andreyev's burly form tackled him by

the ankles and he went down, Banning knew a moment of rage at himself. He had been civilized too long . . . inexcusably careless of him—'Sbones and teeth!

He hit the deck with the other man on top. The red face glared murder. Andreyev yanked at the gun in Banning's kilt with one hand, his other grabbed the arm holding the stun pistol.

Banning brought his hard forehead up, into Andreyev's mouth. The fellow screamed. His fingers released the stunner. At that moment Falken joined the fight, snatching the sleep weapon before Banning could get it into action.

The skipper reached up with an efficiently unsportsmanlike thumb. He had not quite gouged out Andreyev's eye when the man bellowed and tried to scramble free. Banning rolled away. Falken fired at him. An anesthetic dart broke near Banning's nose, and he caught a whiff of vapor.

For a moment, while the universe waltzed around him, Banning accomplished nothing more than to reel to his feet. Falken sidestepped the weeping Andreyev, shoved the captain back against the wall, and yanked the automatic from his waistband.

Cleonie came from behind and threw her arms around Falken's neck.

He shouted, bent his back, and tossed her from him. But it had been enough of a distraction. Banning aimed a kick for the solar plexus. Both guns went on a spin from Falken's hands.

Banning's sole had encountered hard muscle. Falken recovered fast enough to make a jump for the nearest weapon. Banning put a large foot on it. "Oh, no, you don't," he growled.

Falken sprang at him. It was not the first time Banning had been in a party which got rough, and he did not waste energy on fisti-cuffs. His hand snapped forward, open, the edge of a horny palm driving into Falken's larynx. There was a snapping noise.

Falken fell backward, over Andreyev, who still whimpered and dabbed at his injured eye. Banning stooped for the gun.

A bullet smashed down the corridor, rico-cheted, and whined around his ears. Gentry came into view, with the drop on him.

"Oh, oh," said Banning. "School's out." He scooped up Cleonie and scampered back into the companionway.

Up the stairwell! His weight lessened with every jump as he got closer to the ship's axis of spin.

Passing C-deck, he collided with Charles Wayne. The young second mate had obviously been yanked from sleep by the racket. He was pulling on his gold-collared blue uniform jacket as he entered the companionway. "Follow me!" puffed Banning.

Gentry appeared at the foot of the stairs. The automatic in his grasp found an aim on the captain's stomach. "Stay there!" he rapped. "Raise your hands!"

Banning threw himself and Cleonie backward, into C-deck corridor. The bullet snapped viciously past Wayne's head. "Come on, I told you!" gasped Banning. "Get her to the bridge!"

Wayne looked altogether bewildered, but any spaceman learns to react fast. He slung the girl over his shoulder and dashed down the hall toward an alternate stairwell.

Banning followed. He heard Gentry's shoes clang on metal, up the steps after him. As he ran, he groped after his pipe lighter, got it out, and thumbed the switch.

There were rails and stanchions along the wall, for use in null-gravity. Aided by his lessened weight, Banning swarmed ape fashion up the nearest and waved his flame beneath a small circle in the ceiling.

Then down again, toward the stair! Gentry burst into the hall and fired. Coriolis force deflected the bullet, it fanned the captain's cheek. The next one would be more carefully aimed.

The ceiling thermocouple reacted to heat, flashed a signal, and put the C-deck fire extinguisher system into action with a lather of plastifoam. Gentry's second shot flew off to nowhere. Thereafter he struggled with the stuff while Banning scampered up the stairs.

The bridge was a bubble in the ship's nose, precisely centered on the axis of rotation. There was virtually no weight, only a wilderness of gleaming consoles and the great viewscreen ablaze with its simulacrum of the sky.

Cleonie hung on to a stanchion, torn and

shaken by the wretchedness of sudden, unaccustomed free fall. Tetsuo Tokugawa, the
first mate, whose watch this was, floated next
to her, offering an antidizzy pill. Wayne
crouched by the door, wild-eyed. "What's
going on, sir?" he croaked.

"I'm curious to know myself," panted
Banning. "But it's all hell let out for noon."

Tokugawa gave him a despairing look. "Can
you stuff this pill down her throat, skipper?"
he begged. "I've seen people toss their dinner
in null-gee."

"Uh, yeah, it is rather urgent." Banning
hooked a knee around a stanchion, took the
girl's head in one hand, and administered the
medicine veterinary fashion. Meanwhile he
clipped forth his story.

Tokugawa whistled. "What the destruction
is this?" he said. "Mutiny?"

"If passengers can mutiny . . . neat point of
law, that. Be quiet." Banning cocked his head
and listened. There was no sound from the
passages beyond the open door. He closed and
bolted it.

Wayne looked sick. He wasn't a bad young
fellow, thought the captain, but he was
brought up in the puritan reaction of today's
Western peoples. He was less afraid of
danger, now, than stunned by a kick to his
sense of propriety. Tokugawa was more
reliable, being Lunar City bred, with all the
Lunar colonist's cat-footed cosmopolitanism.

"What are we going to *do?*" rasped the
second mate.

"Find out things," grunted Banning. He soared across to the intercom cabinet, entered it, and flicked switches. The first thing he wanted was information about the ship. If that failed them, it would be a long walk home.

The "Thunderbolt" was a steelloy spheroid, flattened along the axis of the drive-tubes whose skeletal structure jutted like an ancient oil derrick from the stern. She was a big ship: her major diameter more than three hundred meters; she was a powerful ship: not required to drift along a Hohmann ellipse, but moving at a speed which took her on a hyperbolic orbit—from Earth Station Prime to the Jovian System in less than a month! But she had her limitations.

She was not intended to enter an atmosphere, but orbited and let shuttleboats bring or remove her cargo. This was less because of the great mass of her double hull—that wasn't too important, when you put atomic nuclei to work for you—than because of the design itself. To build up her fantastic velocities, she must spurt out ions at nearly the speed of light: which required immensely long accelerating tubes, open to the vacuum of space. They would arc over and burn out if air surrounded the charged rings.

She carried no lifeboat. If you abandon ship at hyperbolic speeds, a small craft doesn't have engine enough to decelerate you before running out of reaction mass. Here, in the big cold darkness beyond Mars, there was no escaping this vessel.

Banning tuned in the screen before him. It gave two-way visual contact between a few key points, in case of emergency. "And if this ain't an emergency," he muttered, "it'll do till one comes along."

First, the biotic plant, armored at the heart of the ship. He breathed a gusty sigh. No one had tampered with that—air and water were still being renewed.

Next, the control gyros. The screen showed him their housing, like the pillars of some heathen temple. In the free fall at the ship's axis, a dead man drifted past them. The slow air currents turned him over and over. When his gaping face nudged the screen pickup, Banning recognized Tietjens, one of the two stewards. He had been shot through the head, and there was a grisly little cloud of red and gray floating around him.

Banning's lips grew thin. "I was supposed to look after you," he mumbled. "I'm sorry, Joppe."

He switched to the engine room. His view was directed toward the main control board, also in the axial null-gee state. The face that looked back at him, framed by the tall machines, belonged to Professor Gomez.

Banning sucked in a breath. "What are you doing there?" he said.

"Oh . . . it's you, Captain. I rather expected you to peer in. "The little man shoved himself forward with a groundlubber's awkwardness, but he was calm, not spacesick at all. "Quite a job you did on Falken. He's dead."

"Too bad you weren't in on that party," said Banning. "How are the other boys? Mine, I mean."

"The red-haired man—he was on watch here when I came—I am afraid I found it necessary to terminate him."

"Tietjens and O'Farrell," said Banning, very slowly. "Just shot down, huh? Who else?"

"No one, yet. It's your fault, Captain. You precipitated this affair before we were ready; we had to act in haste. Our original plan did not involve harming any person." The shriveled face grew thoughtful. "We have them all prisoners, except for you there on the bridge. I advise you to surrender peacefully."

"What's the big idea?" growled Banning. "What do you want?"

"We are taking over this ship."

"Are you crazy? Do you know what sort of job it is to handle her—do you know how much kinetic energy she's got, right now?"

"It is unfortunate that Falken died," said Gomez tonelessly. "He was to have been our engineer. But I daresay Andreyev can take his place, with some help from me—I know a bit about nucleonic controls. Gentry, of course, is a trained astrogator."

"But who are you?" shouted Banning. He had the eerie feeling that the whole world had gone gibbering insane around him. "What are you doing this for?"

"It is not essential for you to know that,"

said Gomez. "If you surrender now, you will receive good treatment and be released as soon as possible. Otherwise we shall probably have to shoot you. Remember, we have all the guns."

Banning told him what he could do with the guns and cut the circuit. Switching on the public-address mike, he barked a summary of the situation for the benefit of any crewmen who might be at liberty. Then, spinning out of the booth, he told the others in a few harsh words how it stood.

Cleonie's face had gotten back a little color. Now, between the floating gold locks of hair, it was again drained of blood. But he admired the game way she asked him: "What can we do?"

"Depends on the situation, m'lady," he replied. "We don't know for sure . . . let's see, another steward, two engineers, and a deck-hand . . . we don't know if all four of the crewmen still alive are prisoners or not. I'm afraid, though, that they really are."

"Luke," she whispered. "You sent him off—"

Banning nodded. Even in this moment, he read an anguish in her eyes and knew pity for her. "I'm afraid Luke has been clobbered," he said. "Not permanently, though, I hope."

Wayne's gaze was blank and lost. "But what are they *doing?*" he stammered. "Are they . . . ps-ps-psy-chotic?"

"No such luck," said Banning. "This was a

pretty well-laid plan. At the proper time, they'd have pulled guns on us and locked us away—or maybe shot us. Luke happened to ... I don't know what, but it alarmed Andreyev, who stuck him up. Then I horned in. I sent Luke after help. Not suspecting the other passengers, he must have told Tietjens in the presence of another member of this gang. So poor old Joppe got shot, but apparently Luke was just herded off. Then the whole gang was alerted, and Gomez went to take over the engine room while Falken and Gentry came after me." He nodded heavily. "A fast, smooth operation, in spite of our having thrown 'em off balance. No, they're sane, for all practical purposes."

He waited a moment, gathering his thoughts, then:

"The remaining four crewmen would all have been in their quarters, off duty. The situation as she now stands depends on whether Gentry broke off from chasing me in time to surprise them in that one place. I wish I'd gotten on the mike faster."

Suddenly he grinned. "Tetsuo," he rapped, "stop the ship's rotation. Pronto!"

The mate blinked, then laughed—a short rough bark in his gullet—and leaped for the controls. "Hang on!" said Banning.

"What ... what do you plan to do, sir?" asked Wayne.

"Put this whole tub into null-gee. It'll equalize matters a bit."

"I don't understand."

"No, you've never seen a weightless free-for-all, have you? Too bad. There's an art to it. A trained man with his hands can make a monkey of a groundlubber with a gun."

It was hard to tell whether Wayne was more deeply shocked at the mutiny or at learning that his captain had actually been in vulgar brawls. "Cheer up, son," said Banning. "You, too Cleonie. You both look like vulcanized oatmeal."

There was a brief thrumming. The tangential jets blew a puff of chemical vapor and brought the spin of the ship to a halt. For a moment, the astro screen went crazy, still compensating for a rotation which had ceased, then the cold image of the constellations steadied.

"O.K.," said Banning. "We've got to move fast. Tetsuo, come with me. Charlie, Cleonie, guard the bridge. Lock the door behind us, and don't open it for anyone whose voice you find unmusical. If our boys do show up, tell 'em to wait here."

"Where are you going?" breathed the girl shakenly.

"Out to kill a few people," said Banning with undiminished good cheer.

He led the way, in a long soaring glide through the door. "Up" and "down" had become meaningless; there was only this maze of halls, rooms, and stairwells. His skin prickled with the thought that an armed man might be waiting in any cross-corridor. The silence of the ship drew his nerves taut as wires. He pulled himself along by the rails, hand over hand, accelerating till the door-ways blurred past him.

The galley was on B-deck, just "above" passenger country. When Banning opened the door, an unfastened kettle drifted out and gonged on his head. A rack held the usual kitchen assortment of knives. He stuck a few in his waistband, giving the two longest to himself and Tokugawa. "Now I don't feel so nude," he remarked.

"What's next?" whispered the mate.

"If our lads are being kept prisoner, it's probably in crew territory. Let's try—"

The spacemen's own cabins were on this level; they did not require the full Earth-value of spin-gravity given the passengers on A-deck. Banning slipped with a caution that rose exponentially toward the area he always thought of as the forecastle.

He need not have been quite so careful. Andreyev waited with a pistol outside a cabin door, Andreyev had been unprepared for a sudden change to no-weight. His misery was not active, but it showed.

Banning launched himself.

Andreyev's abused senses reacted slowly. He looked around, saw the hurtling form, and yelled. Almost instinctively, he whipped his gun about and fired. It was nearly point-blank, but he missed. He could not help missing when the recoil sent him flying back-ward with plenty of English.

He struck the farther wall, scrabbled wildly, bounced off it, and pinwheeled to the ceiling. Banning grinned, changed course with a thrust of leg against floor, and closed in. Andreyev fired again. It was a bomb-burst roar in the narrow space. The bullet tore Banning's sleeve. Recoil jammed Andreyev against the ceiling. As he rebounded, it was onto his enemy's knife.

The captain smiled sleepily, grabbed Andreyev's tunic with his free hand, and completed the job.

Tokugawa dodged a rush of blood. He looked sick. "What did you do that for?" he choked.

"Tietjens and O'Farrell," said Banning. The archaic greenish light faded from his eyes, and he added in a flat tone: "Let's get that door open."

Fists were hammering on it. The thin metal dented beneath the blows but held firm. "Stand aside!" yelled Tokugawa. "I'm going to shoot the lock off—can't find the key, no time—" He picked Andreyev's gun from the air, put the muzzle to the barrier, and fired. He was also thrown back by reaction but knew how to control such forces.

Luke Devon flung the door open. The Engineer looked as bleak as Banning had ever known a man to be. Behind him crowded the others, Nielsen, Bahadur, Castro, Vladimirovitch. Packing five men into a cubbyhole meant for one had in itself been a pretty good way to immobilize them.

Their voices surfed around the captain. "Shut up!" he bawled. "We got work to do!"

"Who else is involved in this?" demanded Devon. "Gentry killed Tietjens and took me prisoner . . . herded all of us in here, with Andreyev to help . . . but who else is there to fight?"

"Gentry and Gomez," said Banning. "Falken is dog's meat. We still hold the bridge, and we outnumber 'em now—but they've got the engine room *and* all the guns but one." He passed out knives. "Let's get out of here. We've made enough racket to wake the Old Martians. I don't want Gentry to come pot-hunting."

The men streamed behind him as he dove along another stairwell, toward the bowels of the ship. He wanted to post a guard over the gyros and biotics. But he had not gotten to them when the spiteful crack of an automatic toned between metal walls.

His hands closed on the rail, slamming him to a halt that skinned his palms. "Hold it," he said, very softly. "That could only have come from the bridge."

If we can shoot a door open, I reckon Gentry can, too.

There was only one approach to the bridge, a short passageway on which several companionways converged. To either side of this corridor were the captain's and mate's cabins; at the far end was the bridge entrance.

Banning came whizzing out of a stairwell. He didn't stop, but glided on into the one opposite. A bullet smashed where he had been.

His brain held the glimpsed image: the door open, Gentry braced in it with his feet on one jamb and his back against the door. That way, he could cover Wayne and Cleonie—if they were still alive—and the approach as well. The recoil of his fire wouldn't bother him at all.

Banning's followers milled about like the debris of a ship burst open. He waited till Gentry's voice reached out:

"So you have all your men back, Captain . . . and therefore a gun, I presume? Nice work. But stay where you are. I'll shoot the first head that pokes around a corner. I know how to use a gun in null-gee, and I've got Wayne and Rogers for hostages. Want to parley?"

Banning stole a glimpse at Devon. The Engineer's nostrils were pinched and bloodless. It was he who answered:

"What are you after?"

"I think you know, Luke," said Gentry.

"Yes," said Devon. "I believe I do."

"Then you're also aware that anything goes. I won't hesitate to shoot Rogers—or dive the ship into the sun before the Guard gets its claws on us! It would be better if you gave up."

There was another stillness. The breathing of his men, of himself, sounded hoarse in Banning's ears. Little drops of sweat pearled off their skin, glistened in the fluorotube light, and danced away on air currents.

He cocked a brow at Devon. The Engineer

nodded. "It's correct enough, skipper," he said. "We're up against fanatics."

"We could rush him," hissed Banning. "Lose a man or two, maybe, but—"

"No," said Devon. "There's Cleonie to think about." A curious mask of peace dropped over his bony face. "Let me talk to him. Maybe we can arrange something. You be ready to act as . . . as indicated."

He said, aloud, that he would parley. "Good," grunted Gentry. "Come out slow, and hang on to the rail with both your hands where I can see them." Devon's long legs moved out of Banning's view. "That's close enough. Stop." *He must still be three or four meters from the door*, thought the captain, and moved up to the corner of the stairwell.

It came to him, with a sudden chill, what Devon must be planning. The Rostomily clan had always been that sort. His scalp prickled, but he dared not speak. All he could do was take a few knives from the nearest men.

"Luke." That was Cleonie's voice, a whisper from the bridge. "Luke, be careful."

"Oh, yes." The Engineer laughed. It had an oddly tender note.

"Just what happened to kick off this landslide, anyway?" asked Gentry.

" 'Thou hast the most unsavory similes," said Devon.

"What?"

The roar which followed must have jerked all of Gentry's remaining attention to him as Devon launched himself into space.

The gun crashed. Banning heard the bullet smack home. Devon's body turned end over end, tumbling backward down the hall.

Banning was already around the corner. He did not fire at Gentry; it would have taken a whole fatal second to brace himself properly against a wall.

He threw knives.

The recoil was almost negligible; his body twisted back and forth as his arms moved, but he was used to that. It took only a wink to stick four blades in Gentry.

The spaceman screamed, hawked blood, and scrabbled after the gun that had slipped from his fingers. Tokugawa came flying, hit him with one shoulder. They thudded to the floor. The mate wrapped his legs about Gentry's and administered an expert foul blow to the neck.

Cleonie struggled from the bridge toward Devon. Banning was already there, holding the gray form between his knees while he examined the wound. The girl bumped into them. "*How is he?*" Banning had heard that raw tone, half shriek, often and often before this day—when women saw the blood of their men.

He nodded. "Could be worse, I reckon. The slug seems to've hit a rib and stopped. Shock knocked him out, but . . . well, a bullet never does as much harm in free fall, the target bounces away from it easier." He swatted at the little red globules in the air. "Damn!"

Wayne emerged, green-faced. "This

man . . . shot the door open when we wouldn't let him in," he rattled. "We hadn't any weapon . . . he threatened Miss Rogers—"

"O.K., never mind the breast-beating. Next time remember to stand beside the door and grab when the enemy comes through. Now, I assume you have the medical skills required for your certificate. Get Luke to sick bay and patch him up. Nielsen, help Mr. Wayne. Gentry still alive?"

"He won't be if he doesn't get some first aid quick," said Tokugawa. "You gashed him good." He whistled in awe. "Don't you ever simply *stun* your enemies, boss?"

"Take him along too, Mr. Wayne, but Devon gets priority. Bahadur, break out the vacuum sweeper and get this blood sucked up before it fouls everything. Tetsuo . . . uh, Mr. Tokugawa, go watch the after bulkhead in case Gomez tries to break out Vladimirovitch, tag along with him. Castro, stick around here."

"Can I help?" asked Cleonie. Her lips struggled for firmness.

"Go to sick bay," nodded Banning. "Maybe they can use you."

He darted into the bridge and checked controls. Everything was still off—good. Gomez couldn't start the engines without rigging a bypass circuit. However, he had plenty of ancillary machines, generators and pumps and whatnot, at his disposal down there. The captain entered the intercom cabinet and switched on the engine room screen.

Gomez's pinched face had taken on a stiffened wildness. "For your information, friend," said Banning, "we just mopped up Andreyev and Gentry. That leaves you alone. Come on out of there, the show's over."

"No," said Gomez. His voice was dull, abnormally calm. It gave Banning a creepy sensation.

"Don't you believe me? I can haul the bodies here if you want."

"Oh, yes, I will take your word." Gomez's mouth twisted. "Then perhaps you will do me the same honor. It is still you who must surrender to me."

Banning waited for a long few seconds.

"I am here in the engine room," said Gomez. "I am alone. I have locked the outer doors: emergency seal, you'll have to burn your way through, and that takes hours. There will be plenty of time for me to disable the propulsion system."

Banning was not a timid man, but his palms were suddenly wet, and he fumbled a thick dry tongue before he could shape words:

"You'd die, too."

"I am quite prepared for that."

"But you wouldn't have accomplished anything! You'd just have wrecked the ship and killed several people."

"I would have kept this affair from being reported to the Union," said Gomez. "The very fact of our attempt is more of a hint than we can afford to let the Guard have."

"What are you doing all this *for?*" howled the captain.

The face in the screen grew altogether un-human. It was a face Banning knew—millennia of slaughterhouse history knew it—the face of embodied Purpose.

"It is not necessary for you to be told the details," clipped Gomez. "However, perhaps you will understand that the present government's spineless toleration of the Kali menace in the East and the moral decay in the West has to be ended if civilization is to survive."

"I see," said Banning, as gently as if he spoke in the presence of a ticking bomb. "And since toleration is built into Union law—"

"Exactly. I do not say anything against the Uniters. But times have changed. If Fourre were alive today, he would agree that action is necessary."

"It's always convenient to use a dead man for a character witness, isn't it?"

"What?"

"Never mind." Banning nodded to himself. "Don't do anything radical yet, Gomez. I'll have to think about this."

"I shall give you exactly one hour," said the desiccated voice. "Thereafter I shall begin work. I am not an engineer myself, but I think I can disable something—I have studied a trifle about nucleonics. You may call me when you are ready to surrender. At the first suspicion of misbehavior, I will, of course, wreck the propulsion system immediately."

Gomez turned away.

Banning sat for a while, his mind curiously empty. Then he shoved across to the control board, alerted the crew and started the rotation again. You might as well have some weight.

"Keep an eye on the screen," he said as he left the main pilot chair. "Call me on the intercom if anything develops. I'll be in sick bay."

"Sir?" Castro gaped at him.

"Appropriate spot," said Banning. "Velocity is equivalent to temperature, isn't it? If so, then we all have a fever which is quite likely to kill us?"

Devon lay stretched and stripped on the operating table. Wayne had just removed the bullet with surgical pincers. Now he clamped the wound and began stitching. Nielsen was controlling the sterilizers, both UV and sonic, while Cleonie stood by with bowl and sponges. They all looked up, as if from a dream, when Banning entered. The tools of surgery might be developed today to a point where this was an operation simple enough for a spaceman's meditechnic training; but there was a man on the table who might have died, and only slowly did their minds break away from his heartbeat.

"How is he?" asked the captain.

"Not too bad, sir, considering." Given this job, urgent and specific, Wayne was competent enough; he spoke steadily. "I daresay he presented his chest on purpose when he attacked, knowing the bones had a good chance of acting as armor. There's a broken rib and some torn muscle, of course, but nothing that won't heal."

"Gentry?"

"Conked out five minutes ago, sir," said Nielsen. "I stuck him in the icebox. Maybe they've got revivification equipment on Ganymede."

"Wouldn't make much difference," said Banning. "The forebrain would be too far gone by the time we arrived—no personality survival to speak of." He shuddered a little. Clean death was one thing; this was another matter, one which he had never quite gotten used to. "Luke, though," he went on quickly, "can he stand being brought to consciousness? Right away?"

"No!" Almost, Cleonie lifted her basin to brain him.

"Shut up." He turned his back on her. "It'd be a poor kindness to let him sleep comfy now and starve to death later, maybe, out beyond Pluto. Well, Mr. Wayne?"

"Hm-m-m . . . I don't like it, sir. But if you say so, I guess I can manage it. Local anesthesia for the wound and a shot of mild stimulant; oxygen and neoplasma, just in case— Yes, I don't imagine a few minutes' conversation would hurt him permanently."

"Good. Carry on." Banning fumbled after his pipe, remembered that he had dropped it somewhere in all the hallabaloo, and swore.

"What did you say?" asked Nielsen.

"Never mind," said Banning. True, women were supposed to be treated like men these days, but he had old-fashioned ideas. It was useful to know a few earthy languages unfamiliar to anyone else.

Cleonie laid a hand on his arm. "Captain," she said. Her eyes were shadowed, with weariness and with—compassion? "Captain, is it necessary to wake him? He's been hurt so much—for our sakes."

"He may have the only information to save our lives," answered Banning patiently.

The intercom cleared its throat: "Sir . . . Castro on bridge—he's unbolting the main mass-tank access port."

Wayne turned white as he labored. He understood.

Banning nodded. "I thought so. Did you ask him what he was up to? He promised us an hour."

"Yes, sir. He said we'd get it, too, but . . . but he wanted to be ready, in case—"

"Smart boy. It'll take him awhile to get to the flush valves; they're quite well locked away and shielded. Then the pump has to have time. We might have burned our way in to him by then."

"Maybe we should do it, sir. Now!"

"Maybe. It'd be a race between his wrenches and our torches. I'll let you know. Stand by."

Banning turned back to Devon, gnawing his lip. The Engineer was stirring to wakefulness.

As he watched, the captain saw the eyes blink palely open, saw color creep into the face and the mouth tighten behind the transparent oxygen mask.

Cleonie moved toward the table. "Luke—"

Devon smiled at her, a sudden human warmth in this cold room of machines. Gently, Banning shoved her aside. "You'll get your innings later, girl," he said. Bending over the Engineer: "Hello, buster. You're going to be O.K. Can you tell me some things in a hell of a hurry?"

"I can try—" It was the merest flutter of air.

Banning began to talk. Devon lay back, breathing deeply and making some curious gestures with his hands. He'd had Tighe System training, then—total integration—good! He *would* be able to hang on to his consciousness, even call up new strength from hidden cellular reserves.

"We clobbered all the gang except Gomez, who seems to be the kingpin. He's holed up in the engine room, threatens to wreck us all unless we surrender to him inside an hour. Does he mean it?"

"Yes. Oh, yes." Devon nodded faintly.

"Who is this outfit? What do they want?"

"Fanatic group . . . quasi-religious . . . powerful, large membership furnishes plenty of money . . . but the real operations are secret, a few men—"

"I think I know who you mean. The Western Reformists, huh?"

Devon nodded again. The pulse that flickered in his throat seemed to strengthen.

Banning spent a bleak moment of review. In recent years, he had stayed off Earth as much as possible; when there, he had not troubled himself with political details, for he recognized all the signs of a civilization going under. It had seemed more worthwhile to give his attention to the Venusian ranch he had bought, against the day of genocide and the night of ignorance and tyranny to follow. However, he did understand that the antitechnic Oriental cult of Kali had created its own opposite pole in the West. And the prim grim Reformists might well try to forestall their enemies by a coup.

"Sort of like the Nazis versus the Communists, back in Germany in the 1920s," he muttered.

"The who?" said Nielsen.

"No matter. It's six of one and half a dozen of the other. Let me see, Luke." Banning took a turn around the room. "In order to overthrow constitutional government and impose their will on Earth, the Reformists would have to kill quite a few hundred millions of people, especially in Asia. That means nuclear bombardment, preferably from space. Am I right?"

"Yes—" said Devon. His voice gained resonance as he went on. "They have a base, somewhere in the asteroid belt. They hope to build it up to a fortress, with a fleet of ships, arsenal, military corps . . . the works. It's a very long-range thing, of course, but the public aspect of their party is going to need lots of time anyway, to condition enough citizens toward the idea of— Well. At present their base doesn't amount to much. They can't just buy ships, the registry would give them away . . . they have to build . . . they need at least one supply ship, secretly owned and operated, before they can start serious work at all."

"And we're elected," said Devon. "Yeah. I can even see why. Not only is this a fast ship with a large capacity, but our present cargo, the terraforming stuff, would be vaulable to them in itself . . . Uh-huh. Their idea was to take over this clunk, bring her in to their base—and the "Thunderbolt" becomes another ship which just plain vanished mysteriously."

Devon nodded.

"I scarcely imagine they'd have kept us alive, under the circumstances," went on Banning.

"No."

"How do you know all this?"

"The Order . . . We stay out of politics . . .officially . . . but we have our Intelligence arm and use it quietly." So that was why he'd been reluctant to explain Andreyev's actions! "We knew, in a general way, what the situation was. Of course, we didn't know *this* ship, on this particular voyage, was slated for capture."

"That's fairly obvious. You recognized Andreyev?"

"Yes. Former Engineer, under another

name—expelled   for . . . good   reasons.
Surgical changes made, but the overall gestalt
bothered me. All of a sudden, I thought I knew
who he was. Like a meddling fool, I tried a
key word on him. Yes, he reacted, by pulling a
gun on me! Later on—again, like an idiot—I
didn't think Gentry might be his partner, so I
told Tietjens what had happened while Gentry
was there." Devon sighed. "Old Rostomily
would disown me."

"You weren't trained for secret service
work, yourself," said Banning. "All right,
Luke. One more question. Gomez wants us to
surrender to him. I presume this means we'll
let ourselves be locked away except for one or
two who slow down the ship while he holds a
gun on 'em. After we've decelerated to a point
where a boat from the Reformist asteroid can
match velocities, he'll radio and—Hell! What
I'm getting at is, would our lives be spared
afterward?"

"I doubt it," said the Engineer.

"Oh my darling—" As he closed his eyes,
Cleonie came to his side. Their hands groped
together.

Banning swung away. "Thanks, Luke," he
said. "I didn't know if I had the right to risk
lives for the sake of this ship, but now I see
there's no risk at all. We haven't got a thing to
lose. Cleonie, can you take care of our boy
here?"

"Yes," she whispered, enormous-eyed. "If
there's no emergency."

"There shouldn't be. They fabricated him out of teflon and rattlesnake leather. O.K., then, you be his nurse. You might also whomp up some coffee and sandwiches. The rest of the crew meet me at the repair equipment lockers, aft section . . . no, you stay put, Castro. We're going to burn our way in to friend Gomez."

"But he . . . he'll dump the reaction mass!" gasped Wayne.

"Maybe we can get at him before he gets at the tanks," said Banning. "A man might try."

"No—look, sir. I know how long it takes to operate the main flush system. Even allowing for Gomez being alone and untrained, he can do it before we can get through the after bulkhead. We haven't a chance that way!"

"What do you recommend, Mr. Wayne?" asked Banning slowly.

"That we give in to him, sir."

"And be shot down out of hand when his pals board the ship?"

"No, sir. There'll be seven of us one of Gomez before that happens. We have a faint hope of being able to jump him—"

"A very faint hope indeed," said Banning. "He's no amateur. And if we don't succeed, not only will we die, but that gang of hellhounds will have gotten the start it wants. Whereas, if we burn through to Gomez but fail to stop him disabling the ship . . . well, it'll only be us who die, now. Not a hundred million people twenty or thirty years from now."

*Is this the truth? Do you really believe one
man can delay the Norns? What is your choice,
Captain? By legal definition, you are omni-
potent and omniscient while the ship is under
way. What shall be done, Oh god of the ship?*

Banning groaned. *Per Jovem*, it was too
much to ask of a man!

And then he stiffened.

"What is it, sir?" Nielsen looked alarmed.

"By Jupiter," said Banning. "Well, by
Jupiter!"

"What?"

"Never mind. Come on. We're going to
smoke Gomez out of there!"

The last, stubborn metal glared white, ran
molten down the gouge already carved, and
froze in gobbets. Bahadur shut off the electric
torch, shoved the mask away from his dark
turbanned face, and said: "All right, sir."

Banning stepped carefully over the heavy
torch cables. His gang had attacked the bulkhead from a point near the skin of the ship,
for the sake of both surprise and weight.
"How's the situation inside?" he asked the
air.

The intercom replied from the bridge,
where Castro huddled over the telescreen that
sowed him Gomez at work. "Pump still going,
sir. I guess he really means business."

"We've got this much luck," said Banning,
"that he isn't an engineer himself. You'd have
those tanks flushed out half an hour ago."

He stood for another instant, gathering

strength and will. His mind pawed over the facts again.

The outer plates of the ship would stop a fair-sized meteor, even at hyperbolic relative velocity: it would explode into vapor, leaving a miniature Moon crater. Anything which might happen to break through that would lose energy to the self-sealer between the hulls; at last it would encounter the inner skin, which could stand well over a hundred atmospheres of pressure by itself. It was not a common accident for a modern spaceship to be punctured.

But the after bulkhead was meant to contain stray radiation, or even a minor explosion, if the nuclear energies which drove the ship should get out of hand. It was scarcely weaker than the double hull. The torches had required hours to carve a hole in it. There would have been little or no saving of time by cutting through the great double door at the axis of the ship, which Gomez had locked; nor did Banning want to injure massive pieces of precision machinery. The mere bulkhead would be a lot easier to repair afterward—if there was an afterward.

Darkness yawned before him. He hefted the gun in his hand. "All right, Vladimirovitch, let's go," he said. "If we're not back in ten minutes, remember, let Wayne and Bahadur follow."

He had overruled Tokugawa's anguished protests and ordered the first mate to stay behind under all circumstances. The Lunarite

alone had the piloting skill to pull off the
crazy stunt which was their final hope. He
and Nielsen were making a racket at the other
end of the bulkhead, a diversion for Gomez's
benefit.

Banning slipped through the hole. It was
pitchy beyond, a small outer room where no
one had turned on the lights. He wondered if
Gomez waited just beyond the door with a
bullet for the first belly to come through.

He'd find out pretty quick.

The door, which led into the main control
chamber, was a thin piece of metal. Rotation
made it lie above Banning's head. He
scampered up the ladder. His hand closed on
the catch, he turned it with an enormous
caution—flung the door open and jumped
through.

The fluoros made a relentless blaze of light.
Near the middle of that steel cave, floating
before an opened panel, he saw Gomez. So the
hell-bound Roundhead hadn't heard them
breaking in!

He did now. He whirled, clumsily, and
scrabbled for the gun in his belt. Banning
fired. His bullet missed, wailed and gonged
around the great chamber. Gomez shot back.
Recoil tore him from the stanchion he held,
sent him drifting toward the wall.

Banning scrambled in pursuit, over the
spidery network of ladders and handholds.
His weight dropped with each leap closer to
the axis; he fought down the characteristic

Coriolis vertigo. Gomez spiraled away from him, struck a control chair, clawed himself to a stop, and crouched in it.

Banning grew aware of the emergency pump. It throbbed and sang in the metal stillness around him, and every surge meant lost mass . . . like the red spurting from the slashed artery. The flush system was rarely used—only if the reaction mass got contaminated, or for some such reason. Gomez had found a new reason, thought Banning grimly. To lose a ship and murder a crew.

"Turn that thing off, Vlad," he said between his teeth.

"Stay where you are!" screamed Gomez. "I'll shoot! I will!"

"Get going!" roared the captain.

Vladimirovitch hauled himself toward the cutoff switch. Gomez flipped his pistol to full automatic and began firing.

He didn't hit anything of value in the few seconds granted him. In a ship rotating in free fall, the pattern of forces operating on a bullet is so complicated that practical ballistics must be learned all over again. But that hose of lead was bound to kill someone, by sheer chance and ricochet, unless—

Banning clutched himself to a rod, aimed, and fired.

On the second shot, Gomez jerked. The pistol jarred from his hand, he slumped back into the chair and lay still.

Banning hurried toward him. It would be worthwhile taking Gomez alive, to interrogate and— No. As he reached the man, he saw the life draining out of him. A shot through the heart is not invariably fatal, but this time it was.

The pump clashed to silence.

Banning whirled about. "Well?" His shout was raw. "How much did we lose?"

"Quite a bit, sir." Vladimirovitch squinted at the gauges. His words came out jerkily. "Too much, I'm afraid."

Banning went to join him, leaving Gomez to die alone.

They met in the dining saloon: seven hale men, an invalid, and a woman. For a moment they could only stare at the death in each other's eyes.

"Break out the Scotch, Nielsen," said Banning at last. He took forth his pipe and began loading it. A grin creased his mouth. "If your faces get any longer, people, you'll be tripping over your own jawbones."

Cleonie, seated at the head of the couch on which Devon lay, ruffled the Engineer's hair. Her gaze was blind with sorrow. "Do you expect us to be happy, after all that killing?" she asked.

"We were lucky," shrugged Banning. "We lost two good men, yes. But all the ungodly are dead."

"That's not so good a thing," said Devon. "I'd like to have them narcoed, find out where their asteroid is and—" He paused. "Wait. Gentry's still in the freeze, isn't he? If he was revived at Ganymede, maybe his brain wouldn't be too deteriorated for a deep-memory probe, at least."

"Nix," said Banning. "The stiffs are all to be jettisoned. We've got to lighten ship. If your Order's Intelligence men—or the Guard's, for that matter—are any good, they'll be able to trace back people like our late playfellows and rope in their buddies."

Cleonie shivered. "Please!"

"Sorry." Banning lit his pipe and took a long drag. "It is kind of morbid, isn't it? O.K. then, let's concentrate on the problem of survival. The question is how to use the in-adequate amount of reaction mass left in the tanks."

"I'm afraid I don't quite understand," said the girl.

She looked more puzzled than frightened. Banning liked her all the more for that. Devon was a lucky thus-and-so, if they lived ... though she deserved better than an Engineer, always skiting through space and pledged to contract no formal marriage till he retired from field service.

"It's simple enough," he told her. "We're on a hyperbolic orbit. That means we're moving with a speed greater than escape velocity for the Solar System. If we don't slow down quite a bit, we'll just keep on going; and no matter how we ration it, there's only a few weeks' worth of food aboard and no suspended-ani-mation stuff."

"Can't we radio for help?"

"We're out of our own radio range to any-where."

"But won't they miss us—send high-acceler-ation ships after us? They can compute our orbit, can't they?"

"Not that closely. Too much error creeps in when the path gets as monstrous long as ours would be before we could possibly be over-hauled. It'd be remarkable if the Guard ship came as close to us as five million kilometers, which is no use at all." Banning wagged his pipestem at her. "It's up to us alone. We have a velocity of some hundreds of kilometers per second to kill. We don't have reaction mass enough to do it."

Nielsen came in with bottles and glasses. He went around doing the honors while Devon said: "Excuse me, Captain, I assume this has occurred to you, but after all, it's momentum which is the significant quantity, not speed *per se*. If we jettison everything which isn't absolutely essential, cargo, furnishings, even the inner walls and floors—"

"Tet and I figured on that," answered Ban-ning. "You remember just now I said we had to lighten ship. We even assumed stripping off the outer hull and taking a chance on meteors. It's quite feasible, you know. Spaceships are designed to come apart fairly easily under the right tools, for replacement work, so if we all sweat at it, I think we can finish peeling her down by the time we have to start deceler-ating."

Wayne looked at the whiskey bottle. He didn't drink; it wasn't considered quite the thing in today's West. But his face grew tighter and tighter, till suddenly he reached out and grabbed the bottle and tilted it to his mouth.

When he was through choking, he said hoarsely: "All right, sir. Why don't you tell them? We still can't lose enough speed."

"I was coming to that," said Banning.

Devon's hand closed on the girl's. "What are the figures?" he asked in a level tone.

"Well," said Banning, "we can enter the Jovian System if we like, but then we'll find ourselves fuelless with a velocity of about fifty kilometers per second relative to the planet."

The Engineer whistled.

"Must we do that, though?" inquired Bahadur. "I mean, sir, well, if we can decelerate that much, can't we get into an elliptic orbit about the sun?"

" 'Fraid not. Fifty k.p.s. is still a lot more than solar escape velocity for that region of space."

"But look, sir. If I remember rightly, Jupiter's own escape velocity is well *over* fifty k.p.s. That means the planet itself will be giving us all that speed. If we didn't come near it, we should have mass enough left to throw ourselves into a cometary—"

"Smart boy," said Banning. He blew smoke in the air and hoisted his glass. "We computed that one, too. You're quite right, we can get into a cometary. The very best cometary we can manage will take a few years to bring us back into radio range of anyone—and of course space is so big we'd never be found on such an unpredictable orbit, unless we hollered for help and were heard."

"*Years,*" whispered Cleonie.

The terror which rose in her, then, was not the simple fear of death. It was the sudden understanding of just how big and old this universe which she had so blithely inhabited really was. Banning, who had seen it before, waited sympathetically.

After a minute she straightened herself and met his eyes. "All right, Captain," she said. "Continue the arithmetic lesson. Why can't we simply ask the Jovians to pick us up as we approach their system?"

"You knew there was a catch, eh?" murmured Banning. "It's elementary. The Republic is poor and backward. Their only spacecraft are obsolete intersatellite shuttles, which can't come anywhere near a fifty k.p.s. velocity."

"And we've no means of losing speed, down to something they can match." Wayne dropped his face into his hands.

"I didn't call you here for a weeping contest," said Banning. "We do have one means. It might or might not work—it's never been tried—but Tetsuo here is one hell of a good pilot. He's done some of the cutest braking ellipses you ever saw in your life."

That made them sit up. But Devon shook his head, wryly. "It won't work," he said. "Even after the alleged terraforming, Ganymede hasn't enough atmosphere to—"

"Jupiter has all kinds of atmosphere," said Banning.

The silence that fell was thunderous.

"No," said Wayne at last. He spoke quickly, out of bloodless lips. "It could only work by a fluke. We would lose speed, yes, if friction didn't burn us up . . . finally, on one of those passes, we'd emerge with a sensible linear velocity. But a broken shell like this ship will be after we lighten her—an atmosphere as thick and turbulent as Jupiter's—there wouldn't be enough control. We'd never know precisely what orbit we were going to have on emergence. By the time we'd computed what path it really was and let the Jovians know and their antiquated boats had reached it . . . we'd be back in Jupiter's air on the next spiral!"

"And the upshot would be to crash," said Devon. "Hydrogen and helium at one hundred and forty degrees Absolute. Not very breathable."

"Oh, we'd have spattered on the surface before we had to try breathing that stuff," said Vladimirovitch sarcastically.

"No, we wouldn't either," said Bahadur. "Our inner hull can stand perhaps two hundred atmospheres' pressure. But Jupiter goes up to the tens of thousands. We would be squashed flat long before we reached the surface."

Banning lifted his brows. "You know a better 'ole?" he challenged.

"What?" Wayne blinked at him.

"Know anything which gives us a better chance?"

"Yes, I do." The young face stiffened. "Let's get into that cometary about the sun. When we don't report in, there'll be Guard ships hunting for us. We have a very small chance of being found. But the chance of being picked up by the Jovians, while doing those crazy dives, is infinitesimal!"

"It doesn't look good either way, does it?" said Cleonie. A sad little smile crossed her lips. "But I'd rather be killed at once, crushed in a single blow, than . . . watch all of us shrivel and die, one by one—or draw lots for who's to be eaten next. I'd rather go out like a human being."

"Same here," nodded Devon.

"Not I!" Wayne stood up. "Captain, I won't have it. You've no right to . . . to take the smaller chance, the greater hazard, deliberately, just because it offers a quicker death. No!"

Banning slapped the table with a cannon-crack noise. "Congratulations on getting your master's certificate, Mr. Wayne," he growled. "Now sit down."

"No, by the Eternal! I demand—"

"*Sit down!*"

Wayne sat.

"As a matter of fact," continued Banning mildly, "I agree that the chance of the Jovians rescuing us is negligible. But I think we have a chance to help ourselves."

"I think maybe we can do what nobody has ever tried before—enter Jovian sky and live to brag about it."

From afar, as they rushed to their destiny, Jupiter had a splendor which no other planet, perhaps not the sun itself, could match. From a cold great star to an amber disk to a swollen shield with storm—the sight caught your heart.

But then you fought it. You got so close that the shield became a cauldron and ate you down.

The figures spoke a bleak word: the escape velocity of Jupiter is about fifty-nine kilometers per second. The "Thunderbolt" had about fifty-two, relative. If she had simply whizzed by the planet, its gravitation would have slowed her again, and eventually she would have fallen back into it with a speed that would vaporize her. There was no possibility of the creaking old boats of the satellite colonists getting close to her at any point of such an orbit; they would have needed far more advance warning than a short-range radio could give them.

Instead, Tokugawa used the last reaction mass to aim at the outer fringes of atmosphere.

The first pass was almost soundless. Only a thin screaming noise, a sense of heat radiated in human faces, a weak tug of deceleration, told how the ship clove air. Then she was out into vacuum again, curving on a long narrow ellipse.

Banning worked his radio, swearing at the Doppler effect. He got the band of Ganymede at last. Beside him, Tokugawa and Wayne peered into the viewscreen, reading stars and moons, while the computer jabbered out an orbit.

"Hello. Hello. Are you there?"

The voice hissed weakly from X Spaceport: "Heh, 'Thun'erbolt.' Central Astro Control, Ganymede. Harris speakin'. Got y'r path?"

"To a rough approximation," said Banning. "We'd need several more readings to get it exactly, of course. Stand by to record." He took the tape from the computer and read off the figures.

"We've three boats in y' area," said Harris. "They'll try t' find y'. G' luck."

"Thanks," said Banning. "We could use some."

Tokugawa's small deft fingers completed another calculation. "We'll strike atmosphere again in about fifty hours, skipper," he reported. "That gives the demolition gang plenty of time to work."

Banning twisted his head around. There was no rear wall now to stop his eyes. Except for the central section, with its vital equipment, little enough remained between the bridge and the after bulkhead. Torches had slashed, wrenches had turned, air locks had spewed out jagged temporary moons for days. The ship had become a hollow shell and a web of bracing.

He felt like a murderer.

Across the diameter of the great spheroid, he saw Devon floating free, ordering the crew into spacesuits. As long as they were in null-gee, the Engineer made an excellent foreman, broken rib and all.

His party was going out to cut loose reactor, fire chamber, ion tubes, everything aft. Now that the last mass was expended and nothing remained to drive the ship but the impersonal forces of celestial mechanics, the engines were so much junk whose weight could kill them. Never mind the generators—there was enough energy stored in the capacitor bank to keep the shell lighted and warmed for weeks. If the Jovians didn't catch them in space, they might need those weeks, too.

Banning sighed. Since men first steered a scraped-out log or a wicker basket to sea, it has been an agony for a captain to lose his ship.

He remembered a submarine once, long ago—it still hurt him to recall, though it hadn't been his fault. Of course, he'd gotten the idea which might save all their lives now because he knew a trifle about submarines . . . or should the Montgolfiers get the credit, or Archimedes?

Cleonie floated toward him. She had gotten quite deft in free fall during the time before deceleration in which they orbited toward Jupiter, when spin had been canceled to speed the work of jettisoning. "May I bother you?" she asked.

"Of course." Banning took out his pipe. She cheered him up. "Though the presence of a beautiful girl is not a bother. By definition."

She smiled, wearily, and brushed a strand of loose hair from her eyes. It made a halo about her worn face. "I feel so useless," she said.

"Nonsense. Keep the meals coming, and you're plenty of use. Tietjens and Nielsen were awful belly robbers."

"I wondered—" A flush crossed her cheeks. "I do so want to understand Luke's work."

"Sure." Banning opened his tobacco pouch and began stuffing the pipe, not an easy thing to do in free fall. "What's the question?"

"Only . . . we hit the air going so fast—faster than meteors usually hit Earth, wasn't it? Why didn't we burn up?"

"Meteors don't exactly burn. They volatilize. All we did was skim some very thin air. We didn't convert enough velocity into heat to worry about. A lot of what we did convert was carried away by the air itself."

"But still—I've never heard of braking ellipses being used when the speed is as high as ours."

Banning clicked his lighter, held it "above" the bowl, and drew hard. "In actual fact," he said, "I don't think it could be done in Earth or Venus atmosphere. But Jupiter has about ten times the gravitational potential, there- fore the air thins out with height correspondingly more slowly. In other words, we've got a deeper layer of thin air to brake us. It's all right. We'll have to make quite a few passes—we'll be at this for days, if we aren't rescued—but it can be done."

He got his pipe started. There was a trick to smoking in free fall. The air-circulating blowers, which kept you from smothering in your own breath, didn't much help as small an object as a pipe. But he needed this comfort. Badly.

Many hours later, using orbital figures modified by further observation, a shuttleboat from Ganymede came near enough to locate the "Thunderbolt" on radar. After maneuvering around so much, it didn't have reaction mass enough to match velocities. For about a second it passed so close that Devon's crew, working out on the hull, could see it—as if they were the damned in hell watching one of the elect fly past.

The shuttleboat radioed for a vessel with fuller tanks. One came. It zeroed in—and decelerated like a startled mustang. The "Thunderbolt" had already fallen deeper into the enormous Jovian gravity field than the boat's engines could rise.

The drifting ship vanished from sight, into the great face of the planet. High clouds veiled it from telescopes—clouds of free radicals, such as could not have existed for a moment under humanly endurable conditions. Jupiter is more alien than men can really imagine.

Her orbit on reemergence was not so very much different. But the boats which had almost reached her had been forced to move elsewhere; they could not simply hang there, in that intense a field. So the "Thunderbolt" made another long, lonesome pass. By the time it was over, Ganymede was in the unfavorable position, and Callisto had never been in a good one. Therefore the ship entered Jupiter's atmosphere for a third time, unattended.

On the next emergence into vacuum, her orbit had shortened and skewed considerably. The rate at which air drag operated was increasing; each plunge went deeper beneath the poison clouds, each swung through clear space took less time. However, there was hope. The Ganymedeans were finally organizing themselves. They computed an excellent estimate of what the fourth free orbit would be and planted well-fueled boats strategically close at the right times.

Only—the "Thunderbolt" did not come anywhere near the predicted path.

It was pure bad luck. Devon's crew, working whenever the ship was in a vacuum, had almost cut away the after section. This last plunge into stiffening air resistance finished the job. Forces of drag and reaction, a shape suddenly altered, whipped the "Thunderbolt" wildly through the stratosphere. She broke free at last, on a drastically different orbit.

But then, it had been unusual good luck

which brought the Jovians so close to her in the first place. Probabilities were merely re-asserting themselves.

The radio said in a weak, fading voice: "Missed y' 'gain. Do' know 'f we c'n come near, nex' time. Y'r period's gettin' very short."

"Maybe you shouldn't risk it." Banning sighed. He had hoped for more, but if the gods had decided his ship was to plunge irretrievably into Jupiter, he had to accept the fact. "We'll be all right, I reckon."

Outside, the air roared hollowly. Pressures incomparably greater than those in Earth's deepest oceans waited below.

On his final pass into any approximation of clear space—the stars were already hazed—Banning radioed: "This will be the last message, except for a ten-minute signal on the same band when we come to rest. Assuming we're alive! We've got to save capacitors. It'll be some time before help arrives. When it does, call me. I'll respond if we've survived, and thereafter emit a steady tone by which we can be located. Is that clear?"

"Clear. I read y'. Luck, spaceman . . . over an' out."

Watching the mists thicken in the view-screen, Banning added figures in his head for the hundredth time.

His schedule called for him to report at

Phobos in fifteen days. When he didn't, the Guard would send a high-acceleration ship to find out what had gone wrong. Allow a few days for that. Another week for it to return to Mars with a report of the facts. Mars would call Luna on the radio beam—that, at least, would be quick—and the Guard, or possibly the Engineers, would go to work at once.

The Engineers had ships meant to enter atmosphere: powerful, but slow. Such a vessel could be carried piggyback by a fast ion-drive craft of the Guard. Modifiecations could be made en route. But the trip would still require a couple of weeks, pessimistically reckoned.

Say, then, six weeks maximum until help arrived. Certainly no less than four, no matter what speeds could be developed by these latest models.

Well, the "Thunderbolt" had supplies and energy for more than six weeks. That long a time under two-plus gees was not going to be fun, though gravanol injections would prevent physiological damage. And the winds were going to buffet them around. That should be endurable, though; they'd be above the region of vertical currents, in what you might call the Jovian stratosphere—

A red fog passed before the screen.

Luke Devon, strapped into a chair like everyone else, called across the empty ship: "If I'd only known this was going to happen—what a chance for research! I do have a few instruments, but it'll be crude as hell."

"Personally," said Banning, "I saved out a deck of cards and some poker chips. But I hardly think you'll have much time for re-search—in Jovian atmospherics, anyway."

He could imagine Cleonie blushing. He was sorry to embarrass her, he really did like that girl, but the ragged laugh he got from the others was worth it. While men could laugh, especially at jokes as bad as his, they could endure.

Down and down the ship went. Once, caught in a savage gust, she turned over. If every-thing hadn't been fastened down, there could have been an awful mess. The distribution of mass was such that the hulk would always right itself, but . . . yes, reflected Banning, they'd all have to wear some kind of harness attached to the interior braces. It could be improvised.

The wind that boomed beyond the hull faded its organ note, just a trifle.

"We're slowing down," said Tokugawa.

And later, looking up from the radaltimeter: "We've stopped."

"End of the line." Banning stretched. He felt bone-crushingly tired. "Nothing much we can do now. Let's all strap into our bunks and sleep for a week."

His Jovian weight dragged at him. But they were all alive. And the ship might be hollowed out, but she still held food and drink, tools and materials, games and books—what was needed to keep them sane as well as breathing in the time they must wait.

His calculations were verified. A hollow steelloy shell, three hundred odd meters in diameter, could carry more than a hundred thousand tons, besides its own mass, and still have a net specific gravity of less than 0.03. Now the Jovian air has an average molecular weight of about 3.3, so after due allowance for temperature and a few other items, the result was derived that at such a thickness its pressure is an endurable one hundred atmospheres.

Like an old drop in a densitometer, like a free balloon over eighteenth-century France, like a small defiant bubble in the sky, the "Thunderbolt" floated.

Psychodynamics survived; the Psychotechnic Institute perished. "Hubris, nemesis, ate," wrote one observer. "The tragic flaw in the character of Institute personnel was only that they were human." Civilization outgrew the constrictive matrix that had shaped it, yet it emerged better equipped than ever to cope with the beckoning universe beyond.

As our species moved out among the stars, would we finally learn to master ourselves? Or would all our future victories be cold?